For Christine Z. and all the

other bright souls taken

far too soon.

‘

'It would be a danger – and he shuddered at the thought – if any evil

force, such as a demagogue, should begin to work'.

George R. Stewart – 'Earth Abides'

Ready-Made
Dreams

The dream was disturbing, and though he couldn't recall it, the fading tendrils haunted Lars Quickbreath as he lay sweat-soaked on his futon in the gray morning light.

Little could he know it was to be his last.

He rolled about, burrowing further into the tangle of sheets and pillows when an abrupt screeching drove its way into his brain-pan. The mini-compu/Gov-mon stuttered an amber lambency, bathing the tiny compartment in its ominous glow, indicating the arrival of an official bulletin.

Mandatory.

Lars yawned and crept over the floor to the prefab shelf that served as his desk, smacking lips together, tasting the night and his dream.

Though it was his duty as a citizen to absorb each and every Government dispatch, he'd once calculated the odds of getting tagged or flagged were the notification missed or ignored. There were simply too many people to surveil. Lars still had a better chance of winning the obligatory Fed-lottery each month.

Which he never did.

Still, it was that time anyway.

Pulling the commodity into focus, Lars looked into the fractious face of the new leader, President Archibald Thrette III. Crude real-time rendering failed to mask bovine eyes, set within sagging, pasty flesh. The traditional black Stetson was cocked in a devil-may-care manner, with its starred red, white, and blue band.

"Ma fella Mericans," he addressed Lars in an aggressive southern drawl. "…it is ma sincerest plesha to be befo ya taday, as ya newly elected Chief of State, an ta execute ma first executive orda."

The election. A contemptably corrupted puppet-show that had, after three nepotistic generations, yeilded this person.

"A new an sweepin resalution, designed ta thwaht insarection from ah common enemea, from both within and without."

A fractured thread of images flickered, dissolving from his mind; hidden memories of the dream.

"This new law, which ah have christened Resalution Backslash, is a one-two punch to potential terrorism." The President's face puckered. "Faith Raygistration will be the first orda of business. Each and evera citizen must provide a record of his or her religious beleifs. Enrollment must be in person. You will need a valid picsha I.D. and will be

3

given a variety a options ta select from." Eyes squinted atop the pucker. "*Atheism* is *not* a choice."

Lars shook his head. So he was to register his belief in something he didn't believe?

"Secondly, anea form of literature oa communication that is not in electronic oa streamin' foamat, anathing that cannot be monitad oa tapped is now prohibited. These tracts, these documents can and do hold ideas dangerous to society, the nation, and ta *you*. "

Lars blinked. *Books.* He's talking about banning books. He eyed long rows of titles marching accross his shelves.

A smile stretched the Thrette's face. "People, bewae the *educated* man. Trust not the *intellectual*. Have faith onlea in the *Bable*. Believe onlea in *Jesus*."

Lars was frozen, chilled by the lunacy of this man's words.

"…special drop-off sahts bein implemented in neighbahoods all around oua beloved countra. In return, special tax credits will be issued." The smile was gone now, and he smacked a tiny fist into his palm, a strangely effete gesture. "It is oua dutea, as citizens of this great nation and as sevants unda oua *Lord God*, ta rid ouaselves of this potentially subvesive material. Ah have generously granted a moratorium of nan months foa voluntary compliance." Inhaling deeply, rapturously, the President locked a feral look onto Lars.

"Now…let us pray…"

Christ, Lars thought, with just his first act, he'd defiled both the Constitution and the Bill of Rights. What next?

He rose, stepping into the shower cube, leaving the President babbling prayers to the empty room.

*   *   *

5

Downtown, on his way to work in South-Central Mid-City, Lars noted the increased presence of Centurions, black and silver uniforms peppering the dense crowd of civilians with a nearly even ratio; straight-shaved military haircuts, thick necks, massive arms; men and women morphing into a homogenous mass of androgynous muscle. Even among supposed citizens, he spotted an uncountable number of undercovers in business suits, eyes squinting around the room over papers and pads pushed up before them.

He became more acutely aware than usual of his conspicuous appearance. The ratty dreadlocks tied up behind his head contrasted greatly with current hair-trends for men; shorn sides with that gelled, wavey-scallop thing up top, woman appearing to gravitate towards a genus of conservative compact bouffant.

Up ahead, two Stylish ladies in business suits doted over a German shepherd held at bay by a uniformed cop. Lars had once heard these dogs could only be trained to sniff out a single substance, not a range of them. If that were true, he hoped this one was a bomb-sniffer. He'd half a tobacco cigarette hidden in his delivery satchel, and though it was wrapped well against the smell, it still caused him concern: the penalty for possession of an illegal narcotic was a Federal Offense.

Holding breath, he stepped out into a denser section of the crowd as it flowed down the hall, but both officer and dog were caught up in the attention of the girls.

The bicycle delivery service he worked for was located in the basement of the INFLO high-rise, but he stopped first at the Start-Rite Cafe stationed near the elevators. Pungent, acidic aromas hung in the air, assaulting his sinuses, provoking immediate nausea. He handed over his monthly ration card to the twitchy, wild-eyed girl behind the counter, digging in his pocket for the few wrinkled bills that remained. Pushing a large thermal cup to Lars with convulsive motions, a smile snapped on her lips with recognition.

"Hi Lars, hi. *Howyoubeengettingreadyforanotherdayonthestreet?*"

She seemed to vibrate, little spasms rippling through arms and legs. He searched his memory for her name.

"Hey Lemon…yeah, livin'n the dream, y'know?."

Her arm shot out like a whip, the speed of a karate move, snatching bills from his outstretched hand, aiming them at a laminated sign on the wall.

"*See?* Paper money's only good through the end of the year. After that, we can only take plastic."

"What? " he croaked. Before him the girl actually began bouncing up and down as the smells, the sounds crashed into him. Taking a deep breath, he closed his eyes, gripping the edge of the counter, willing them open again.

"Hey, Lars, you allright? Need a double shot espresso?" She leaned into his field of vision, ripples of concern twitching over her face.

"Nah… think I just need some air. You know, *fresh*. See you later Lemon."

"Ya. Ciao, Lars." The smile rubberbanded back in place and she shot across the counter to the next customer.

In the subterranean hallway, where he was sure no one could observe, Lars tossed the full cup of coffee into the trash. God, he hated the stuff, but Fedlaw demanded a three cup-per-day minimum, something to do with supporting the Government's South American business interests.

He swiped his I.D. through the card slot of the security door, heard the heavy locks clack open and stepped through to the converted loading dock that housed the delivery service. A mushroom of tight-packed brown curls dipped out the dispatch window.

"Hey Quickbreath, you got…" Gibbons, head dispatcher, blinked eyes wide beneath his hair portobello. "…*jeez*, wrong side of the bed?"

"Could say that."

"Hear the prez this morning?"

"It's the law, Gibbons. I have to hear."

"Fucking hilarious."

"Hilarous…?"

"Yeah, he's pretty entertaining, right? I think this guy's actually going to get some things done."

Lars' molars were grinding. "Oh yeah. He's definitely gonna be doing some things."

An arm attired in a peculiarly textured shade of green stuck out the window for emphasis. Looked like a puppet.

10

"Come on, Quickbreath, since when have any of the President's policy's ever really affected *our* lives?"

Maybe so, but what about all the people who will *be impacted?* Lars said nothing. Explaining empathy to one who has none was futile. "Gotta grab my ride."

The puppet arm disappeared; returned with a pink card. "Got your first drop here."

"Shit Gibbons, give a guy a chance to punch in."

Deneb Shaula was hanging by the time card machine. He took in her lithe, muscular form, accented by the distressed camo shorts she favored, sculptural planes of her face complimented by a close cropped bristle of black hair. She turned.

"Lars, you look like shit."

"Morning to you, too." He slid his card as the machine did an impression of the security door, registering date and time. Deneb crossed her arms, offering a quizzical look.

"No, I mean it. Let me guess, …late night? Hot date? Late night with a hot date?" Muscles and tendons rippled along arms as she see-sawed them over her chest.

"I *look* like I'm glowing with satisfaction? Nah, think it's this dream I had. Can't shake it, but can't remember it either… you know?"

She stopped and frowned. "That's weird. Same thing with me last night."

"Yeah?"

"Yeah."

He let his eyes roam up and down her figure. "So why you look all hot-as-love and shit?"

Deneb flashed a killer smile, finger briefly brushing his lips. She about-faced, shooting him a look back over her shoulder.

"Cause I always look hotter-than-love?"

He watched her walk away, comically wagging ass, sounds of her combat boots echoing down the hallway.

"True dat." he muttered to himself.

"Ah swear!" Lars jumped. Chank's voice was uncomfortably close to Lars' ear.

"If ah wasn't a woman trapped in a man's body, ah'd wanna be a man with *that* woman's body!"

Chank was a six and a half foot, two-hundred fifty pound mass of muscle that happened to be a coffee-skinned blond transgender. He/she also had a fondness for overstated feminine gestures.

"Chank, you scared the shit…"

"*Oh. My. God.*" Chank punctuated each word with a paw to Lars' chest. "Honey, you look like shit."

"Yeah, I heard."

"Lars, sweetie, you just tell Chanky every-little thing."

"Okay? For one, stop poking me."

Chank's hands fluttered over his chest. They stopped; hung in the air between them. "Is it the Thrette's statement?"

"That *fucktard*!"

"Shush, honeypie." Chank's enormous arms guided him away to an unmonitored corner in the hallway. "The ears in the walls have holes. Holes, *knowwhatimsaying?*"

Lars let out a long sigh. "I just don't care anymore."

"Well, sweetie, you should." The inflection deserted Chank's voice, eyes looking down with concern. "You know, this place is one of the few left that will let our little rag-tag family of misfits be. The shit comes down here? Hell, I'd be on the streets again. Or worse, in the workhouse." Chank's shoulders shuddered with a flourish. "Now I know about that precious fiction collection of yours…"

"Aw, it's not about that." Lars scratched his head. "Or maybe that's part of it? I don't know. Shit, that fucked-up dream …"

Inked eyebrows jumped up on Chank's forehead. "Funny you should mention that …"

*   *   *   *

A little girl's hand reaches out and turns a doorknob. She pulls open the door as a plume of smoke rushes out, and a horrified expression crosses her face.

"Mommy!" She cries.

In the reaction shot mom turns, horrified, holding a cigarette, trying to blow smoke out a cracked window. She drops the butt into the toilet bowl.

"Oh, Katrina…" Little puffs of smoke punctuate her words as she kneels down beside the child. "… I'm so sorry. Mommy's …

addicted to tobacco." She looks up to her daughter for forgiveness.

"Mommy needs help…"

The man is obviously intoxicated.

He weaves down a dark street, glancing off walls when he encounters a police officer, apparently busy with something else. The man drunkenly couples wrists together before him and implores to the officer:

"I've been drinking alcohol. Will you arrest me?"

A couple is driving recklessly, car swerving left and right through the frame, each laughing manically as they smoke from sinister looking pipes. Headlights slash across the windshield as the woman leans into the man violently kissing him on the neck. He drops the pipe in his lap and his crazed laughter turns to alarmed yelping as he desperately gropes around the seat. The screech of tires on asphalt grows in volume; a moment after they exit the frame, there is a loud crash.

Smoke, hissing liquid sounds, and the tinkling of cracked glass fade over a new scene …

The couple lie inert on the dashboard, the windshield a web of cracks. The man rouses himself slowly to consciousness, blood running from nose and mouth, crowd of people gathering around. He looks dazed, remorseful, and appeals to the person next to him:

"We've been doing drugs. Would you please contact the authorities?"

Another member of the crowd turns around, Lars recognizing him from small parts in numerous B-movies, slowly shaking his head in disgust. He addresses the camera:

"Let's face it, impaired people just aren't going to turn themselves in. The only way to find them is by cracking down, from coast to coast. It doesn't matter where you live, we'll find you."

Dramatic music resonates over bold, colorful graphics as a deep, somber voice intones:

"This message has been brought to you by the Homeland Intelligence Agency..."

*　　*　　*　　*

That night Lars sat back in his compartment and tried to follow the game, some Federally mandated amalgam of hugely overpaid testosterone cases mindlessly chasing a ball around a fluorescent green field, but the ceaseless roar of the hive-mind and the announcer's hysterical caterwauling chafed his brain.

He shut down the Hitachi, listening to noises from the compartment above. The thud of footsteps and sounds of furniture scraping across the ceiling traced the architecture of an argument; he could hear the muffled chorus of yelling even through the heavy insulation.

Oddly enough, Lars was lulled by the sounds, falling into an early, deep sleep, watching phosphene patterns that crawled around within his eyelids.

*   *   *   *

Awake the next day, he felt rested and refreshed, his mind steam-cleaned and pressed without the murky aftertaste of the previous night's dream. Even the sun seemed to conspire, putting in a rare appearance during his commute to work, bringing sharpness and contrast to the morning.

Lemon was nowhere to be seen at the coffeehouse, and that put him in such a good mood that he actually considered drinking the stuff, but the oily, hot-tar smell turned his stomach, and he covertly got rid of it.

On impulse he stopped at the Smacky-Snack Market to grab a bite for breakfast. Row upon row of compact, densely packaged, single-serve products presented themselves, bathed beneath the sickly-green 60 cycle hum of fluorescents. He pulled down a miniature bag of Kettle Mom's Organi-chips and the small L.E.D on the ident-tag winked redly at him.

"Thank you, sir or madame, for choosing a Kettle Mom product." The bag's androgynous A.I. voice sounded tinny sqeaking out the microspeaker.

"It's sir." Lars said to the bag.

"Excuse me, sir." One of the competing brands opposite the aisle was winking its own amber pinpoint of light. "Why not choose Rancho Deluxe brand chips, eighteen dee-licious flavors, now with thirty percent more flavo-boost."

"I like the Organi-chips." Lars glanced around, uncomfortably. "I've had them before."

"The customer has made his choice." The bag in his hand stated with mock pride.

"You're the customer." The little amber light darkened, and Lars started down the aisle toward the checkout counter.

"Kettle Mom's also has twelve other mouth-watering flavors, including a variety ..."

"Shut up. You're just a fucking bag of chips."

"You're the customer." The bag quipped cheerfully, and shut down.

Unlike the coffee shop, the market's counter was deserted; behind it sat a small ebony man solemnly looking at the headlines of an old-fashioned newspaper. He glanced up with troubled eyes as Lars approached.

"Why do they smile?" His voice was soft and thickly accented. "They want to kill people, but still they smile."

Lars peered down at the blocks of photographs of the president and the grinning members of his cabinet beneath headlines that boasted some new military action in a country he had never even heard of. *Jesus*, another war? He must've slept through that statement. How many did that make now? Was this lonely clerk's family in that poor country right now?

Were things always this deranged? He couldn't seem to remember, but the fact that he was reacting this way indicated something was amiss. Why couldn't he remember?

The clerk's soft brown eyes still held him, and he shrugged. "Ah...I don't know. Maybe they smile because they're ...*insane?*" He barked a harsh, embarrassed laugh, but the clerk merely nodded in agreement ...

*   *   *   *

"Now *that's* the Lars we all know and love!" Chank's voice boomed around the cavernous interior of the former loading dock, calling Lars' arrival to the attention of all the other messengers. "Child, you look three-hundred percent better."

"Thanks, slept like the dead." He smiled in spite of himself at Chank's latest display of wearable debauchery. Black leggings beneath a red sarong, featuring a blazing gold dragon. A leather bodice created a cavernous cleavage against which chattered the beaded ends of cornrows, the look topped off with a battered gray pair of Chuck Conners. "Hey, you smell good."

"You like? Called Hunter-Seeker." Chank gave a twirl that gave motion to the skirt and beads. "Gonna give it a try at the Flamin' Oh tonight."

"That where you hang, huh?"

"That's where *we* hang tonight." Deneb squeezed between the thicket of bodies, slipping her arm through Chank's, taking Lars in. "Mmm... don't you just look good enough to eat this morning." The tongue piercing clicked against her teeth.

"Yeah, …um, morning Den," Lars could feel the flush rising up his face. "…like the hair." The ends of her jet-black shocks now glowed bright red.

"Thanks." She quilled the spikes with similarly emblazoned fingernails. "Care to join us tonight?"

"I dunno. A place called the Flamin Oh?"

Chank snorted. "The man just ho-mo-phobic."

"I'm not afraid of homos," Lars enjoyed these verbal sparrings with Chank. "…just don't like places with questionable bathroom accomidations."

"Told you the man was ho-mo-phobic." Chank and Deneb exchanged a complex handshake.

The room shifted sideways a few inches. A concussive thump hammered the basement like the footfall of a giant, shattering a plate-glass window in the dispatch office, throwing Lars against the wall with the force of a punch to the chest. Somewhere, someone screamed.

"Shit, that was close!" He and Chank pulled Deneb up from the floor where she had fallen. "Den, you all right?"

"Uhn, …yeah, gotta get my breath back."

And he was running through the security door, up the dark staircase, out into the bright morning haze of the building's broad plaza.

Cars were stopped at crazy angles as people milled listlessly, shuffling about the streets and sidewalks covered in confetti-like debris, eyes dead; glazed with shock. A few blocks to the north hung an ominous coiling black cloud, infinitely reflected back and forth between the glass canyons of the high-rises. The air was filled with dust and flotsam wafting around currents and eddies of the gusty street, and the occasional sound of a heavier object impacting on cement or glass punctuated the otherwise silent scene.

A pretty young zuppy woman walked unsteadily in his direction, her expensive business suit and fashionable haircut coated in gray ash. Terror filled eyes met his as she held out something small and shiny.

"Is this…is this…" Her voice a dry croak and then she stumbled and the object in her hands fell to the pavement before him.

With the clarity of a nightmare, he observed the human toe, the carefully manicured cuticle, the nail polished and trimmed, white shard of bone poking through glistening red stump.

Lars felt the mechanisms of shock settle over him. Distantly he heard the woman make a choked hiccup sound. When he looked up, she threw up on his boots.

*　　*　　*　　*

A young man enters the room, handsome and stalwart in a crisp blue military uniform, epilates and chest blazing in thick gold stitching. He wears a confident, cocky expression, and his buddies, one black, one white, dressed in chic civilian clothes, receive him warmly. He runs his fingers briskly across the brim of his cap as his friends gather around.

Black guy: "So, what's it like over there?"

White guy: "Yeah, see any action?"

He flashes his friends a brief condescending look, then considers better.

"Nah, it's a lot like here, only…" He considers his response. "…different."

His friends share a look and glance back in reverence.

White guy: "C'mon then, tell us, what is it you do? Ride in a tank…?"

27

Black guy: [excitedly interrupting] "Yeah, do you get to fly in helicopters and launch missiles?"

He sighs and gives them a patient smile. "Nothing like that. I'm a computer operator."

White guy: [incredulously] "Computer operator? Like here?"

The camera dollies slowly into Our Hero's face, cross-dissolving in a sepia-toned montage of him in field camo's cross-cut rapidly as curt instructions are directed by the captain leaning over his shoulder. Commands are given via keyboard, and in an impressive graphic display, the enemy is vanquished. The soldiers all share high-fives and the scene dissolves again into Our Hero's face. He's shaking his head, smiling smugly.

"No. Definitely not like here."

Brash military music intercedes as his image washes into the motto; Army/Air Force Reserves. A gravelly voice-over intones; "Make a choice. Make a difference."

A meticulously rendered bald eagle swoops down from a pillowy, multi-hued sky brandishing razor-sharp talons. It ululates a terrifying screech and morphs into the Presidential Seal.

This, in turn, morphs into the President.

"Citizens, it is with a heavea haht that ah stand befo ya. Thea ah two things wayin in on ma mind tonat. The first concerns the deadlea act of cowahdice that occurred today in Mid-City. This latest terrorist bomin has alreada claimed the lahves of two-hundred twenteah-seven innocent, God-fearin citizens of this great countrea. This cravin attack has, again, been claimed by ASOL, a splinta group of the small, hostile nation whea oua troops ah currentlea engaged in a crucial militarea operation." Pause. "The time of inaction is ova. This is a clear sahn we must step up oua game, hit back stronga."

The president spread arms, encircling the lectern, raising face to the heavens.

" Ma grandad usta say, evera cloud has a silva lanin, and indeed, thea is good news with the bad. Today, we saw the successful deployment of a classified project ma own fatha enacted; the Obital Nuclea Ahsenal Netwak, oa O.N.A.N., as we lak ta call it. This system is an epic technological leap foawad, and carries both defensive and offensive capabilities. This, ma people, is the relization of a *dream* of two genarations."

Jump-cut to close-up; the Thrette's eyes gleam with emotion.

"Let us pray…"

"Balls." Lars shut the Hitachi down and set about the dismal task of packing his collection into thermo-flex boxes. Each title passing through his hands a flicker of recognition, memories of the worlds existing between the covers.

Something peripheral interrupted Lars' thoughts. He glanced back at the Hitachi, feeling cold claws of shock for the second time that day. The jittering crimson L.E.D. on his Gov-Mon meant only one thing.

He'd been flagged.

What the fuck happens now? He tasted the bitter tang of adrenaline, mind racing through scenarios: a warning, a ticket, arrest or incarceration. All were possible he supposed, but none seemed probable.

And really, what had he done? Lars moved across the room, dampness spreading around his armpits. He checked the unit for any further information. Nothing. Nada. Just the goddamn flag signal.

The paperback dropped from his grasp as he sagged to the futon, the long day finally slamming into his body and mind.

Even so, he found it nearly impossible to sleep.

At least there were no dreams.

*   *   *   *

The following days, weeks, passed in a turbid haze of work, sleep, work, the flagging drifting to the back of Lars' mind with all the other anxieties incubating there; small gray worms wriggling about the subconscious.

*   *   *   *

Metallic morning sun oozed onto the crowded plaza, cutting crisp police uniforms now dominating the general populous. Lars felt eyes crawling over him from everywhere, really noticing for the first time nests of security cameras jutting from any and all possible angles, growing like virulent forms of fungus. Breaking every sightline hung blazening monitors perpetually playing scenes of carnage; images from the war, violent street riots, natural disasters, and always, the President, emphatically gesticulating before beating multi-hued banners.

Involuntarily, he locked eyes with a Centurian who held his gaze with malicious scrutiny, and Lars ridiculously found himself struggling to act normal.

His legs seemed to have lost their natural rhythm, arms jittering out of sync with his breathing.

Thinking about breathing was a bad idea.

Dammit, this is absurd, he thought, I haven't done anything wrong. Yet, in his mind's eye, he saw himself spasmodically twitching and gasping as he moved past the cop.

At that moment an aural cacophony of blips, screeches, and jingles cascaded throughout the teeming square, all pagers, cee-phones, talkies, and various communication devices sounding off simultaneously. The Centurian reached for his squawking shoulder-set with perfect mindless Pavlovian response, and Lars breathed an inward sigh of relief, stepping gingerly past, ignoring the racket from his own talkie.

Hackorrists. Pranksters taking advantage of the newly centralized Government Communications Network, disrupting service, often unleashing potent virals to crash some unfortunate's system. Unfortunate, that is, only if responded to. Although occurring almost weekly, citizenry, being mindlessly addicted to their technology, appeared powerless from stopping themselves.

*   *   *   *

Deneb was hanging around the entrance of the shop where she and the rest of the couriers kept their cycles in lock-up. Lars slotted his ident-card through its mechanism. She sauntered up as he freed his bike from its dock, tips of her spiked hair now a neon green.

"*Hey*, Lars." She trailed a lacquered green nail with a tiny red pentagram over his bike's seat.

"Mornin Den." He thrust a capped cardboard mug out. "Do me a favor and drink this shit, will you?"

"Oooh, coffee." She took the cup, inhaling deeply. "What flavor?"

"Does it matter?"

"Nuh. Addicted to the stuff."

"Yeah, you and the rest of the human fucking race."

Her eyebrows wriggled over the rim. "Something bent?"

"Nah." Lars glanced around the room, the former loading dock bristling with morning activity, bikers securing their parcels and packages. "Think I'm losing it is all."

"Mmmm?" Behind a sip. "You know, maybe you should get out more." Her voice went hoarse. "Maybe *we* should get out."

Lars swallowed a couple times to get the wet back into his mouth. "Yeah?"

"Yeah." She sipped, blinking into his eyes. "Give me a call tonight, after work. If you don't already have plans, that is."

"Uh, yeah? I mean, no. That would be great."

Her attention shifted; Lars shuddering as a large hand landed on his shoulder.

Den smiled. "Chank babe, where you been? You're late."

Chank slid over to a nearby wall, cornrows sluicing air between them. "You skinny white boys always so jumpy."

"Yup, every last one of us. Wonder why."

Deneb gasped at the swollen bruise that covered Chank's right eye. "Holy shit! Chank? What the fuck?"

"Chanky had a run-in with the special po-lice last night. Little crack down at the Flamin-Oh."

"Shit, your lip too." Lars fingers investigated his own. "You OK?"

Chank's eyes rolled up at the security monitor mounted opposite the wall. "Prob'ly not the best place to talk about it. You kids just get on to work, and don't worry 'bout me. Chanky can take care of himself. Herself? Myself."

Chank's mass moved past them down the hallway, Deneb's gaze following. She turned back, concern crossing her face. "Lars, what the hell is going on?"

"Don't know, but I don't like it." He felt the lens of the security monitor burning over his shoulder. He whispered. "Don't like it at all."

*   *   *   *

The day had gone bone gray, as had all faces Lars passed as he knifed through city traffic, and on some entropic level he sensed a gestalt of despair. Attentions drawn inward, each involved in acts of self-distraction; head-phones, cee-phones, palm-phones, dependant on a self-reciprocating system of technology. A barrier to the very reality they were searching.

For some reason, the image of a snake eating its own tail struck his mind.

Crossing one intersection, he was startled by the scream of locked-up tires as a white van very nearly T-boned his bicycle. A doughy, grizzled face flopped out the window, pulling a cee-phone from his ear, shaking it out at Lars.

"Hey fuck! Watch where the fuck you going!"

Lars stopped, sighed, and turned to regard the guy's glazed, vapid eyes. He pointed to the pole that poked out of the concrete next to him. "This is *your* stop sign. *You* nearly killed *me*!"

The man blinked once, twice, phone still pointed like a handgun. "*Fuck you*. Next time, I *do* fuckin kill you, cunt!"

Lars bowed with a flourish. "Very nice. Very civilized." He thrashed off quickly before the asshole had time to retort.

The singular thing that kept him from snapping at times like these, or at least today, was the prospect of seeing Deneb later that night. The downside of this being the uncountable carnal fantasies that squeezed between every practical thought or higher brain function. They corkscrewed their way into his frontal lobe, multiplying there, insisting upon playing themselves out to each of their unlikely conclusions. A distracting and tiring enterprise;

obviously a set-up by his own mind for severe disappointment.

It was out of one of these piques of mental masturbation he found himself four stories above street level in the badly ventilated shaft of a skyway, confronted by the broken and frail specter of Angel, an acquaintance of Lars' from further back than he could remember. Angel was wrapped in what appeared to be rags, strumming a beat-up acoustic guitar, his loud and often off-key vocals resonating throughout the chambers of the skyway. The mobile vulgus seethed their way around him, a battered guitar case splayed at his feet, coated by a thin sheen of distressed hard currency.

Lars pushed his way up to the cold shaft of sunlight that haloed his friend. "Angel, hey, it's Lars."

"Ah, dreamer." Without a break in his strumming, Angel's eyes turned in his head and Lars found himself reflected within dilated, bloodshot orbs, informing him that his friend was definitely not of a legal mindset.

"What the fuck you doin', Angel? You know you could be arrested?"

"It's alright bro, I'm not really here." Key shift on the guitar.

"Yeah, you're telling me." He could actually smell tobacco mixed with the sweet, cloying reek of what he strongly suspected was alcohol. This was a very illegal situation here, not improved by the attention they seemed to be garnering.

"Listen, you got to cut out of here."

Angel held a chord, acoustics of the place magnifying and multiplying it as his strumming hand clamped down on Lars' forearm.

"No, you listen." Pulling him in to see the shattered, missing teeth behind his smile. "You got to remember what you've forgotten, understand?"

The sound, a crackle-hiss-pop, jump-started Lars' heart, glance down the corridor confirming his worst fears; a squad of brick-shouldered Centurions intercoursing the annex doorway, crew-cut heads swiveling on thick necks, searching.

"*Fuck* Angel." Lars yanked his hand free, searching pockets, throwing a single bill into the guitar case. "Sorry. You're on your own." He slipped into foot traffic, current carrying him away, another anonymous face in the crowd, hearing Angel's voice boom above whispers leaking from headsets and cee-phones.

"Remember brutha! Remember!"

Before breaching the building doors, Lars chanced one last quick glance over his shoulder. He almost wasn't surprised to see Angel gone.

*   *   *   *

"I'm sorry Lars, really, I am, but I just feel like total shit tonight."

Some interference in reception kept skewing Deneb's face sideways across the screen of the Hitachi, but Lars could see the dark circles under her eyes, the once straight green spikes of hair now drooping heavily. "What was that noise?"

"Just another domestic upstairs." Lars deadpanned. "Or next door. Or both. Hard to tell anymore."

Actually, it sounded more like a couch dropped by a helicopter onto his building.

"Oh." Deneb's lips streaked into a digital demon's snarl, then snapped back again to her weary face. "Well… can we do it another time?"

"Yeah. Sure Den. Hope you feel better." He managed a smile. "See you tomorrow."

"Yup. Nite."

"Nite." Lars hit the end button and smashed his forehead on the counter.

Shit.

The pressure in his groinal area throbbed in syncopation to the noises emanating from the walls and ceiling of his compartment. He grabbed a wad of toilet tissue from the bathroom, some battered, over-viewed porn, and prepared to Get Down To Business. Kneeling there on his floor, listening to the hysterical voices and churning furniture was all very distracting, taking way too long, and when finally he did release, his seed kind of oozed out in a thin dribble accompanied by an uncomfortable and unfamiliar feeling. Looking down in horror, Lars saw his right nut do a slow rollover and stop halfway up in his scrotum.

Herniated testicle.

Fuck.

Fuck.

Fuck.

*   *   *   *

Consciousness crashed in from the silent void, a concrete tsunami of thoughts and images, of light and sound. The room twisted and spun, fragmented shards that gradually settled, coalescing into the drab compartment that boxed in Lars' drab life.

He found himself standing in the bathroom staring at his sink basin. The chrome fixtures had accumulated layers of toothpaste flecks and dried soap scum, concentrated on certain surfaces into intricate organic patterns he'd begun to understand were complex coded semaphores in which were locked certain universal truths. The basin itself grew a veined patina of oxidants, a dull red that webbed from the lines of caulking to where it joined the wall. The floor sprouted a sparse forest of discarded hair, thickening as it encroached the base of the toilet, follicles turning thick and curly, cemented to the tile by stratums of amber tinted scum; the bowl a cancerous cavern encircled by sinister and unnatural colors.

Try as he might, Lars couldn't remember how he'd gotten here. The whole experience of waking and walking into the bathroom simply didn't exist. Edited or erased, a jump-cut in reality. What was happening here?

Without dreams to cushion the transition between deep-sleep and sentience, each morning was a repeated trauma to his psyche.

It had been at least a half year since the last.

Who has stolen my dreams?

A bizarre and disturbing question. He considered the person staring back at him through the cloudy, cracked mirror, noting with alarm the wildness in the eyes, the growing bruises beneath them.

Dreams couldn't be stolen, could they?

With effort he pulled from his trance. An Official Bulletin had the Hitachi's amber light blipping wildly off the walls, stinging his optic nerve. Lars fingered sleep crust from his eyes as the Government feed caught, scrolling over the small screen.

"It is ma unfortunate duta, as yoa elected leada, ta repoat several dahk occurrences that have transpiad within the last twenteah-fouah houahs."

Something struck Lars as odd about the Thrette's image. Nothing obvious or immediately discernable. Things seemed slightly askew on a subliminal level, like the way his tie didn't really match his suit. Or the angle of the Stetson off his forehead; the shadows it threw over his face. Was that it? He leaned in closer, mesmerized.

"Earlia today, anotha horrific act of babarism took the lahves of sixta-six blessed souls in oua great nation's capitol, a sadistic and evil attack claimed again by ASOL. Samultaneous occurrences against oua peace-keepin troops entrenched within multiple sovereign provinces have also caused great suffaing. Complicity is suspected."

His furiously fluttering eyelids kept derailing Lars' train of thought.

"Ah strongla urge oua allies in the U.N, ta join us, ta take action in this struggle against a rising taad of evil."

That was it. The eyes in the shadows.

"Theah's is a sinfully false idolatry. Oua's is the one true God. Oua faith will prevail. Foace will be met with greata foace, and these infidels will be made ta pay foa thea crimes against oua peoples, oua beliefs, and oua nation. Anea individual, group, oa province cooperatin, oa conspirin' with these heathens will be considered treasonous actions, and dealt with as such."

The Threttes's fist crashed down onto the desk sending a convulsion throughout his body, canting the Stetson back on his head to reveal shocking dark pouches beneath the shutterbugging eyes.

"As of this moanin, the terror alert has been advanced to its haest level: crimson. Effective tonat, a ten o' clock curfew will be enfoaced nationwide until ah deem the threat ta be neutralized. People …" Lars was transfixed by a dried fleck of spittle caught in the corner of the President's mouth. "…ah realize that these measures may seem extreme, but oua precious and fragile freedoms ah at stake hea. Ah promise, that with oua faith and oua resolve, standin togetha as one, we will prevail."

So there it was. Martial law. The burgeoning police state was now complete.

A blizzard of tiny black speckles swam before his vision as Lars moved through his morning regimin in a haze of half-formed thoughts, dimly aware of the pain in his lower abdomen.

*   *   *   *

"This is a test. This is only a test. For the next sixty seconds, we will be conducting a test of the Emergency Broadcast Network. "

The familiar mandala of the test pattern covers the Hitachi's screen, but something isn't right. Indeed, as Lars stares at the diagram, there appears to be amorphous blobs, nearly invisible, slithering, writhing behind the graphic, as though living creatures were trapped in that electronic nether-world, attempting to communicate.

The image crackles with static, shifting abruptly, and they vanish, test pattern replaced by the words 'Please Stand By'. The announcers voice returns:

"Had this been an actual emergency, you would have been informed of where to tune for more information ..."

*   *   *   *

"Y'all don't talk much, do ya?"

The all-too-familiar voice startled Lars out of his fugue and he found himself on the light-rail to work face-to-face with none other than the President himself.

"Shit." He glanced about him at the drab, preoccupied faces inhabiting his car, but none registered any evidence of recognition.

"*See* m'boy…" The Thrette leaned in, adjusting the Stetson on his head. Lars smelled the medicinal odor of mouthwash masking something foul. "shit. A singula, vernacula word, whose meanin carries nothin." He made a small gesture. "That ain't communicatin"

"You can't be here." Lars managed a hoarse whisper. "You're not really here." He desperately scrutinized again the passengers lolling about in their seats to the motion of the train. Looking back, an elderly woman beneath a bouffant of turquoise-blue was regarding him with deep-set eyes.

"Young man, I most assuredly am here." Her fingers were claws clutching bags crowding her, drawing them closer. "Are *you* all right?" Concern and fear radiated from her proximity, but the moment was broken by the thunderous crackle from a sortie of low-flying jet fighters. They flashed briefly overhead, afterburners punching at the train's Plexiglas.

The woman jolted up in her seat and a surprised little "oh" popped out her livery lips.

"Don't worry," Lars sighed, wiping cold sweat from his forehead. "…it's just the war."

*　　*　　*　　*

The battered bill lay lonely and uncontested on the counter, the ancient President engraved on it's face looking out through the folds and wrinkles with resignation, as if he were aware the ethics and principles he'd protected in life had all recently been compromised.

Lemon hovered over it, sucking in her cheeks, drumming the counter with cracked and chewed fingernails. She chuffed out a hard sigh, and when she finally looked up, Lars saw beneath her twitching eyebrows the same dark circles, the same look of acute exhaustion he saw everywhere.

"Lars…"

"Lemon, I have to the end of the week. It's still money." He pushed the bill closer but she made no attempt to pick it up.

"But everyone else has made the switch-over." Her voice raised to a plaintive whine, fingernails picking up the tempo. "You're the only one left."

"I don't care."

"But…"

White sparks erupted within his head. "It's still good. It's still legal. You have to take it. Now give me my cup of *HOT BOILED SHIT!*"

Whunk! The bill disappeared and in its place sat the cardboard container, his ration card balanced on top.

"Lars, really, you don't…" But he had already vanished into the morning rush.

The entryway to the Smacky-Snack Market stood boarded up, a heavy switchback gate tightly locked against the plywood. The cleanup must've been swift but hasty. Constellations of safety glass winked from corners of the hallway, and the battered aluminum frames of the store's doors told their own tale.

Lars found himself thinking of the soft-spoken proprietor and pushed the thoughts from his mind.

*   *   *   *

"Hey Gibbons. Tuesday night, right? Your bowling league?"

The dispatch office looked like it had suffered a mild hurricane, desk cluttered in orders, reqisitions, pyramids of coffee mugs, nearly burying his own Hitachi. Gibbons himself was shockingly disheveled, bruising beneath his eyes pronounced. Lars noticed his socks disdn't match.

"Fucking goddamn curfew."

"Still find him hilarious, Gibbons? Are you still, what was it…entertained?"

"Fuck you, Quickbreath."

*   *   *   *

"Hey, look, sorry about last night. It's just…" Deneb paused, pulling on her riding gloves. "…what's with the limp?"

"Uh, stubbed my toe this morning."

"Yeah? Hurt?"

"Not too bad. How you doing?"

She shrugged her shoulders. "So-so. Trouble with sleep. It's weird…" Looking up, Lars was alarmed to see a rare desperation in her eyes. "…I always have such vivid dreams, and usually I remember them. *Lars…*" He caught a thin note of hysteria. "…I can't remember having a single dream since *before the election.*"

Lars was taken aback. He was trying to frame a reply in his mind when Chank pulled another appearing act.

"My, my. Ain't you just two peas in a pod. How *are* my two favorite delivery slaves this fine morning?"

Deneb huffed an imaginary strand of hair from her face. "Well, Lars is limping around like a stray dog, and I seem to be missing my dreams."

"Dreams, huh?" Chank went distant, gazing absently about the room. "Why the limp Lars?"

"Aw, you know, old war wound."

"Yeah, things can be a bitch."

Deneb tip-toed up on her boots to scrutinize Chank's face. "Looks a lot better today. Swelling's almost gone."

"Shit girl, had worse good times." Chank regarded them with a sudden intensity. "Gotta slide, kiddos. Pri-ority package needs to be ASAP." In an uncharacteristic gesture, Chank locked hands with each of them, flashed a sly wink, and slipped off down the hall.

Lars caught Deneb's quizzical glare and shrugged back at her. He deftly pocketed the folded square of paper that Chank had palmed him.

*   *   *   *

The intersection of 407th Street North and Ballard Avenue was infamous among bicycle couriers for a variety of reasons. Aside from carrying some of the heaviest two-way automobile traffic in the city, it also served one of the light-rail's central station hubs, channeling thousands of pedestrians onto the sidewalk per day. Compounding this was the presence of several major loading docks intercoursing heavily-trailored delivery trucks, their drvers attempting to maneuver the lumbering giants into ridiculously small locations, bottlenecking and backing up traffic. It was a place where tempers flared and accidents flourished.

Lars straddled his bike beneath totem-pole traffic lights and checked his watch. The slipstream of a double bus tugged at him, wheezing and snorting its way by, and he pulled the note from his pocket to double-check it. Four simple words were printed there:

NEED TO TALK. SAFE!

That, with this address and time.

The light changed and he steeled himself for another wave of foot traffic, when Deneb veered ahead of the mob and stopped, front tire kissing his. Pushing up dark wraparounds she leaned close over the handlebars, shouting above the melee. "Fancy meetin' you here."

"Indeed."

Then the throng was upon them, a blizzard of human Brownian movement, buffeting arms and shoulders, sharp elbows, disjointed faces. Bracing against the signal pole, Lars clasped Deneb's bike to his, she doing likewise as the storm thickened, then suddenly abated.

Standing there, cycle forming a triad with theirs, was Chank, smile perched between glittering cornrows.

"So glad you could make it."

Lars guffawed. "Christ, you got to teach me that shit."

Deneb dipped her head. "I just wanna know how you ride with those bellbottoms."

"Trade secret, child. I tell you, I'd have to kill you."

"So why we here?"

Chank eyed them curiously. "Well, there you go. I suppose you've heard of the curfew?"

Lars bristled. "It's martial law, Chank."

"That it is. That. It. Is."

"So what the fuck about it?"

Chank assessed the next wave of pedestrians building across the street. "I think it's time Chanky came clean to you two about a few things. But not here. Not now."

"What you talkin about?"

"Jesus Lars, don't you hear?" Deneb eyed the gathering crowd with apprehension.

The din of a low-flying military transport added a booming bass line to the street's dissonant soundtrack, its shadow an angel of death riding down the high-rise canyons, and Chank had to lean over to be heard.

"Alright you two, listen. This Friday I want you to meet me. At midnight. That means breaking curfew. That means breaking martial law. Now, you OK with that?"

Deneb snorted. "You kidding?"

"Where you want us?"

Chank's expression was oddly solemn. "1313th Street South, Aramchek Avenue East. Memorize it."

Lars consulted his mental map, shook his head, checked it again. "Chank, that's the heart of Blackout District. Dead Zone."

"You bet your sweet booty it is." The green walking man signal switched on with a soft thunk. "Gotta proj kids. No more until then." Chank executed a neat twist-flip and shot off down the sidewalk.

Deneb finger-combed her sharp shocks, bristling them like porcupine quills. "What the fuck we getting into here?"

"I…" But he was cut off by the sea of humanity lurching and seething around them.

*   *   *   *

They were waiting outside his compartment door as he arrived home from work.

The man was tall, gaunt, clean-shaven. His short blond hair had that cut currently in style Lars now thought of as The Beaver Tail; woman short, stocky, and mean-faced, her crew-cut military style salt and pepper. Both cloaked in long gray overcoats.

Lars' heart hammered double-time in his chest as the man spoke:

"Lars Quickbreath?"

"Who wants to know?"

They pushed out wallets that flipped open revealing chromium badges. "People for United Democracy. I'm Field Agent Kakner and this is Lieutenant Vachel."

Lars examined the official looking insignia, glancing back up in disbelief. "P.U.D. You call yourself PUD? That's...that's just...."

Kakner sighed. "Please Mr. Quickbreath, can we discuss this inside?"

"Don't you need a warrant or something?"

Lieutenant Vachel spoke; "Mr. Quickbreath, this is not a criminal situation. We merely wish to discuss a few things with you. However, if you continue to be uncooperative, we can obtain a search warrant in a matter of minutes." She held out some sinister species of portable gadgetry and he caught the malicious glint behind her eyes. "It would not look very good, though."

"So who's being uncooperative?" Lars threw up his hands. "Come on in. My place is your place."

He shot the lock-slot and led them in, his compartment barely large enough to accommodate the three of them. He gestured toward the single chair perched near the counter. "Uh, have a seat."

"Please Mr. Quickbreath, sit down. We prefer to stand."

"Of course." Lars dropped himself in the chair and crossed his arms. "So, you guys cops?"

Kakner strolled over to the counter on his right while Vachel remained near the door, flanking him, probing black eyes taking all in with snapshot blinks.

"We represent a branch of Homeland Intelligence Agency."

"Hiya."

"Correct."

"So you *are* cops."

"In a manner of speaking."

"Well, you gonna tell me what this is all about?"

Kakner picked Lars' Hitachi off the counter, turned it over with thin, pale fingers, consulting another ominous looking device he produced from somewhere deep inside his coat. "Government issue computer slash monitor slash telecommunication device, Hitachi model number 4072 serial number 03510013 slash 396. Can you confirm that this is yours, Mr. Quickbreath?"

"Well, I haven't memorized the serial numbers, but since the thing's been with me for…I dunno, forever, I'd have to say yes."

Lieutenant Vachel's fingertips flew over a replica of Kakner's gadget. "On March 13th of this year, at precisely O' seven hundred hours central-standard time, the President gave a mandatory address on the terror situation. Your G.C.M.T.V.C. did not receive it."

"G.C.M.T.V.C.?"

Kakner waggled the Hitachi in front of Lars' nose. "This."

"Oh. Hey…"

"In addition, during the President's subsequent address the following evening, your unit cut out only two minutes into the broadcast." She glared at him with outright hostility. "Is your G.C.M.T.V.C. unit malfunctioning?"

"Well, no…"

"There are no records of any repair calls."

"Whoa, wait a sec guys. I was upset. I mean, I…I was at the bombing and I saw a fucking toe," Lars felt hysteria well up inside him as the experience leaked back. "...then this chick barfs all over me..."

"You saw the bombing?" Kakner exchanged glances with Vachel.

"Yeah. Well, no. I got there right after, and the smell... and the bodies..." His voice cracked as he curled into the chair. Kakner hunched down, resting a reassuring hand on Lars' shoulder.

"Mr. Quickbreath. Lars. We're not the bad guys. We're here to help. We understand that there is to be a certain amount of mitigating circumstance, and it's our job to route out that information."

But Lars could not stop himself from babbling. "How can everyone catch every address? I mean, people got to work, they got to sleep, got to shit, It's impossible..."

Kakner patted Lars shoulder. "All this has been taken into consideration. It's not impossible. It's a system that works."

There was a muted crash from upstairs followed by frenzied screeching and Kakner jumped back on his feet. "What the hell was that?"

Lars let out a long shuddering sigh as he felt emotion and tension drain, and he sensed that he'd passed some crucial juncture with these two field operatives.

"*That* would be my neighbors."

It was Lieutenant Vachel's turn to show concern. "You ever call the police on these domestics?"

Lars choked on a bitter laugh. "You kidding? I'd have to call the cops if they stopped."

Field Agent Kakner's attention shifted over Lars' shoulder. "Say, that's quite a collection of fiction you got back there."

"Yeah, I know, I know. But I still got time before, you know…"

Lieutenant Vachel was typing furiously on her device and looked up. "So why the procrastination?"

Lars shrugged. "I'm still reading 'em?"

Kakner picked up one dog-eared volume with the tongue of a book-marker sticking out. "Hmm. Kafka's The Trial?"

"Good book."

"You know, the irony is not lost on me Mr. Quickbreath."

"Um."

Vachel humphed at something on her screen and stepped closer, the look of sour distaste on her face even more intense, if that were possible. "You certainly masturbate quite above what the Bell Curve defines as normal, Mr. Quickbreath."

"Wha-what? You can't…"

"It's simply not healthy."

"Christ." Lars gripped the sides of his chair in impotent rage.

"Are you a religious man, Mr. Quickbreath?"

Lars turned his attention back to Kakner and quelled the desire to scream, to smash the chair he was sitting on over Vachel's buzz-cut head, to do anything. "You can't ask me that."

"We can ask you anything."

"But I don't have to answer."

"True." Kakner looked sad. More typing. "What can you tell us about Eugene Rhybys?"

"Eugene what?"

"You probably know him as …uh, Chank."

"Chank's name is Eugene?"

"What can you tell us about him?"

71

"Chank's a transgender."

"A what?"

"Not a he or a she. Both."

"Oh." He scowled at his screen and seemed genuinely confused. "Anything else?"

"I work with Chank." With an effort, Lars released his grip on the chair and massaged his aching fingers. "Hell of a good cyclist."

Agent Kakner shared a look across the room with Lieutenant Vachel, probably communicating on some super-secret police E.S.P. bandwidth. Each in turn folded their screens in on themselves and returned them deep into the recesses of their overcoats. They moved in the direction of the door.

"It appears that we have concluded our business here, Mr. Quickbreath." Lars moved out of the chair and held the door open, trying to conceal the relief he felt as they started out. "Thank you for your cooperation."

Here it comes.

Kakner turned as if he'd heard the thought. "One more thing …have you noticed anything, er, unusual about your dreams lately?"

Lars tried to look bored. "Dreams? Like what?"

"Oh, you know, any changes in frequency or intensity."

"Nah," Lars lied. "…same old dreams. Same old nightmares."

Kakner was trying too hard to be casual about the issue, and even if he sensed the lie, to pursue it would concede it's importance, and Lars was struck by a sudden certainty that that was the last thing they wanted to do.

"All right Mr. Quickbreath." The intensity of his gaze belied the indifferent tone of his voice. "Have a good evening. And get rid of those books. We'll be following up on that."

"Field Agent Kakner?"

"Yes?" They'd had to turn around again, and Lars caught a faint edge of annoyance in his reply.

"You ever think about the Government survelling *your* sex life?"

"I'm an agent *of* the Government, Mr. Quickbreath."

"My point. My point exactly." And just before he shut the door, Lars had the satisfaction of seeing doubt cross both their faces. And something else.

Fear.

*   *   *   *

Sleep did not find him easily that evening. Outside, the city was eerily quiet as a result of the curfew, which, in turn, only succeeded in defining the aural activities of his neighbors to an unbearable degree. The small singular window projected a surreal cinema over the landscape of the ceiling, and Lars lay on his back contemplating the lightplay, feeling anger and outrage burn deep and hot within his psyche. Dark and vulgar fantasies manifested themselves between intersecting angles of the walls and ceiling as the depravities of his neighbors reached his ears.

He lay there wishing for sleep, praying for the release of dreams.

Prayers that fell on deaf ears.

The following morning he mentioned nothing of his visit by the two field agents to either Deneb or Chank. Indeed, each of them seemed distant and removed themselves, their interactions reduced to monosyllabic responses and distracted glances. Whether it was out of a desire not to discuss their upcoming meeting openly, or if they, too, were struggling with similarly distracted perceptions as his own, he couldn't tell.

*   *   *   *

Early that Friday, at a familiar intersection, Lars felt his cycle buck and swerve sideways, the peal of rubber on asphalt shrieking in his ears. He managed to control the bike to a stop adjacent the driver door of a white van.

The exact same van at the exact same intersection.

Sticking out the window, the drivers stubbled jowls trembled in outrage beneath moribund eyes gleaming with hatred; cee-phone framed against one ear, middle finger stuck in its opposite.

The world went dim and silent as time stopped.

The bike slid to the pavement between his legs in the middle of the street. Stepping over, Lars felt muscles, toned from years of physical labor, coil into rock.

Still holding the cee-phone, the man threw the van into park. He shouted over the half-open window, reaching inside for the door handle. "I told you, cunt, next time I fucken…"

Before he was conscious of his actions, Lars' leg shot out, boot popping through the glass, connecting heavily with the man's jaw, throwing him up, head slamming off the ceiling with a meaty sound, where it disappeared inside. The cee-phone clattered to the pavement at his feet. A white-hot core of anger burned unquenched as he kicked the door concave, hearing a voice screaming; "*Empathy, …empathy!*" then realizing it was his own.

Thin murmurs floated from the phone as he put the receiver to his lips and spoke; "I fucked your wife." Then, for good measure, he smashed it to dust on the van's rim.

As an added bonus, it appeared that his testicle had finally descended.

*   *   *   *

The darkened towers and skyscrapers of Blackout District loomed portentous against a pewter night sky, back-lit faintly enough by the distant city lights to discern their jagged shapes, rising, like decayed and broken teeth seen from within a leviathan's grin.

Years ago, this had been a thriving upscale sector of the city, a center of finance and commerce. Before prohibition it was rumored to have been the entertainment and nightclub district. Naturally, it had become an ideal target for terrorists, striking with such relentless frequency as to render all attempts at reconstruction futile. Whole buildings, then whole blocks were condemned, until finally the entire zone was abandoned; shut down. Now bordered on three sides by industry and south by super-highways, Blackout District was virtually walled in. The dark cancerous tumor in the heart of the gleaming Magna-City.

Earlier, Lars had cycled nearly twenty miles to the outskirts to wait out the intervening hours beneath Cross-Country 1's titanic overpass. The rhythmic thrumming of traffic had lulled him into a dreamless nap, and he woke several hours later, in darkness, disoriented but refreshed.

For stealth's sake, Lars kept mostly to the alleys, shadows concealing thicker shadows, flickering and darting about, driving him forward in primal adrenaline rush.

Now he encountered a collapse, big old-time brick and mortar, its rubble standing a good three stories over the alley. He'd had to backtrack around, using the main streets, feeling instantly vulnerable and exposed. The darkness and silence was a crushing vacuum, so unlike his regular life; so bleak and alien he actually felt homesick for the bright, noisy compartment.

.   Like any good courier, he knew exactly where he was, though this was his first visit. Aramchek Avenue had to be coming soon.

An opaque, rubbery form slid along his peripheral, scuttling through the gloom. Lars jacked into high, kicking hard, tearing up the remaining blocks in haste.

Rounding a corner Lars was struck by a sense of déjà vu so great it had him reeling. Like he'd been here before, seen this, not just once, but a million more.

The building's monolithic edifice rose thirty stories, etched against the stygian sky. Its gothic construction contrasted greatly to the surrounding crystalline glass towers, panes of which had long since surrendered themselves to urban entropy, yawning vampire grins of broken shards twinkling in the dim twilight.

He walked the bike slowly forward, click of free-wheel echoing like gunshots down the silent avenue.

There was a dry scuffling as two forms separated from inky shadows near the base of the building.

"Why, sweetie, you look like you seen a ghost."

Crossing the rubble-strewn courtyard in the muted, monochrome light, Chank and Deneb did indeed resemble ghosts.

"All right, Eugene, time to spill it."

Chank's eyebrow dipped. "*Hmmm.* Ears in the walls been doin some talkin?"

Deneb shucked hands in her back pockets; looked up at Chank. "Eugene?"

Lars joined them. "Coupla' Government affiliates. Asked a lot of questions. Seemed interested in you."

"Eugene?" Deneb giggled.

"Didn't choose it child, you know?" Chank sighed and pulled out a cee-phone the size of a ration card, delicately tapping out an impossibly long stream of numbers with fingers far too large to perform the task. . "Not exactly a positive development. Need to check with my man on this."

Pause... Chank spoke quietly into the mouthpiece. "Me babe. We here." A nod; Chank terminated the connection, acknowledging the two of them.

"So."

A rank, warm breeze slid down the avenue. Lars followed converging lines of the building towering above, to where it cleaved the night sky. Tiny pinpricks of light; aircraft and satellites, blinked and boiled above, behind.

"Chank? What *is* this place?"

"This is the underground."

Deneb tipped her chin up. "It's a skyscraper, Chank."

"Figure of speech."

Rusty thunder of metal on metal tore into the silence. A gleaming crimson eye winked open near the foundation, bathing the steps in hard, red light. Lars jumped at the sound, Deneb pressing into him as the gnarled shadow of a mutant monster splashed down the stairs, lurching and writhing, reaching the flickering light at their feet.

Frozen with terror, Lars felt Deneb's hand slide into his as they stood there, stupidly waiting for the creature to clear the doorway, to savage them. The shadow oozed over their bodies, onto their faces.

Silhouetted against the doorway appeared a small man, head canted upon crooked shoulders, hobbling excitedly towards them with a pronounced gimp. As he neared, they could see thick glasses beneath greasy strings of black hair windshield-wipering with each awkward step.

Lars released the breath he'd been holding as Deneb sagged against him. She slipped her hand from his with an embarrassed fleck of her eyes.

Chank spoke calmly beside them. "Lars. Deneb. I'd like you to meet my man, *the* man. Dante."

Dante stood before them, mouth-breathing noisily. A smile quivered on his lips, his hands quivered side to side, and pretty much all else of him quivered as well. He seemed unable to determine which to address. Suddenly two small sweaty hands shot out, enclosing Lars' right, pumping it vigorously, glasses sliding to the tip of his nose.

"Yes… ah, yes. Lars Quickbreath, Such a pleasure to meet you." Fingers found his glasses and pulled them back up.

. "Mr. Dante," Lars cocked his head. "...do I, ah , know you?"

Dante looked over at Chank, fingers twiddling before his chest. "You haven't told him?"

"That be your area of expertise, darlin."

"Oh... ah, yes. Of course. And Deneb Shaula," He pulled in her hand and pumped the glasses back down his nose. "...you are every bit as beautiful as Chank has described you."

Deneb hissed lightly at his touch but smiled politely. "Well, thank you, Mr. Dante. Pleased to meet you too." She reflexively wiped her hand against her shorts.

Dante fingered the glasses back up, blinking through them at Chank.

There was a silence that was the void of Blackout District.

Chank shrugged. "Your show."

"Oh… ah, yes." Dante shuffled a couple of steps back, and wrapped in the red glow of the doorway, threw both small arms up in a grand gesture. "Welcome to Hell…" he giggled at his own joke.

"…I'll be your guide."

Deneb gave Lars a sideways glance, twirling forefinger around her temple, universal symbol for cuckoo.

*   *   *   *

The fluorescent fixture in the cavernous cargo elevator sputtered and popped as it groaned unsteadily upward. The four of them were braced along various points of the thing's superstructure as it abruptly canted and swayed.

Deneb set her boots in a wider stance. "You sure this thing is safe?"

Chank snorted. "Hasn't dropped me yet."

"Great."

Lars turned to Dante. "You call this place Hell. Just curious. Why?"

His thick glasses magnified the shuddering green light. "Well... ahm, we live in a world of contradictions, Mr. Quickbreath. Black is white, up is down..."

"Heaven is Hell."

"Precisely. You see, Hell here is the embodiment of things lost." He sighed sadly, and Lars was touched at how much emotion such a simple gesture could convey.

"You're both far too young to remember, and it's not something you're apt to find in any history files, but this nation actually used to be a shining beacon of freedom and hope in a dark and tumultuous world. We stood as an example of the potential of the individual in society, one of our primary tenets being the right to pursue happiness. The remainder of the world viewed us with both admiration and jealousy; we were the richest, most intelligent, most technologically advanced culture in human history, but absolute power *always* corrupts, and we had all the power in the world."

Dante turned his face to the wall, voice becoming so hushed Lars and Deneb had to strain to hear.

"A terrible thing happened, a test, perhaps, and instead of rising to the call, we reacted blindly, allowing the infection of fear and corruption to overwhelm our leadership, and the pollution of disinformation to corrupt our media plagued lifestyle. The small freedoms were the first to suffer."

He turned back, an angry quaver in his voice. "Things done here are illegal, yet ironically it is the pursuit of these same principles that formed the basis for our so-called free society, so very long ago. These things were taken from us in barely discernable increments under the auspices of safety, protection, national security, or whatever opportune crises the Government could take advantage of, to bring us to the sad state of affairs we exist in today." Gasping, winded by his oration, Dante sucked in a couple of raspy breaths, sliding lenses back up, continuing.

"Me and a number of… ah, colleagues created Hell as a means to rediscover those original ideals, perhaps in hope of inspiring some sort of tactile spirituality, divine inspiration, if you will, in a society largely bereft of it." He fiddled with a console on the wall and the elevator lurched to a stop.

"Your floor, Chank."

Deneb's eyes went wide. "You leaving us?"

Chank pulled up the safety gate and took her hands. The parting cargo doors filled the cabin with pulsing vermillion light and the distant sub-sonic pulse of music. "Chanky needs to meet some friends and take a load off. Just stick with my man, here. You in good hands."

She nodded, parting their grasp, glancing over at Lars with uncertainty.

Chank whirled, took two steps into the hallway, stopped and turned to face them again, eclipsing the doorway. "One more thing Dante?"

His fingers twiddled over the console. "Ah … yes Chank?"

"Our Mr. Quickbreath here was visited by a couple of Fed's the other evening. Asked 'bout me by name. Don't know what it means, but I thought you should know."

"Oh… my. Well. I don't know." Dante's whole small form went strangely still. He finally raised his face to the ceiling, washing it in the stuttering glare of the fluorescent. "Quantum will need to be consulted on this."

Chank grunted, waving a hand. "*Ta,* sweeties. After your little talk, you bring them back down to the Styx, Dante. We show them what Hell is *really* about."

Dante quivered back into motion. "Um… yes. Of course."

The gate crashed shut and they resumed their tenacious upward crawl.

"The Styx?" Lars nodded at the gate.

"A nightclub. Chank's favorite and I believe… um, the most popular in Hell."

Deneb came off the wall. "But nightclubs are…"

"Illegal, yes." Dante's arms snapped up from his sides and attempted to encompass the entire building. "Please understand the architecture of our dichotomy. For simplicity sake, we'll say that Hell operates on three basic levels, the lower ones being dedicated to the stimuli of the corporeal, of the body. There you will find workout and training facilities; meditation, martial arts, yoga, various individual sports, adult entertainment..."

"Pornography?"

"*Down boy.*" Deneb barked.

"...um, yes, very high production values, everything from print to holographic. Brothels and bathouses as well. Then there are the drug labs..."

"*Drug labs?*"

"Down girl."

"...oh yes. Hydroponic farms growing tobacco, cannabis, poppy, coca, and all the necessary engineering to refine them."

"Ho-lee shit."

"Does this... ah, offend you, Mr. Quickbreath?"

"Well, no. It's just..." Lars tried to run fingers through his dreadlocks, getting them tangled, throwing up his hands instead. "...just trying to wrap my head around all of this."

Dante nodded. "The central levels are dedicated to the cultivation of the mind, the… ah, more creative pursuits. The Arts. Painting, sculpture, literature, music. We have wonderful audio-visual facilities and the most comprehensive library in the nation."

"Books. You got books."

"Well, yes. That would… um, define a library."

"Third level?"

"Science, philosophy, religion. Concerns of the… ah, soul?"

The elevator thundered to a stop and they lingered as echoes boomed themselves into silence around them. Deneb leaned against the battered wall, cocking her head.

"And on what level do your… ah, concerns place you, Mr. Dante?"

Dante's smile was a peculiar thing perched below that face. "Why, the penthouse, of course."

They followed the sparse hallway around the central elevator shaft, the minimal geometric planes awash in pools of light from ancient overhead sconces, to a simple, small door. Dante scuttled out in front, turning to face them, fingers twiddling nervously with limp strings of hair.

"You must understand, um… very, *very* few people have seen this." Within the wall there was a thick clack and the door swung slowly open with an exaggerated grandeur, revealing how much more massive it was than it appeared. They waited for the sheer depth of the door to clear it's jamb, and when Lars finally was able to step inside, it took a few moments for him to comprehend what he was seeing.

He whistled in appreciation. "O.K. You've piqued my interest."

The room opened out, tiering down several levels, wrapping around to both the left and right, appearing to circumscribe the entire structure, broken only by thick concrete support pilings. Surrounding the entire room, and, he assumed, the entire floor, where the windows would have looked out over the city, stood an unbroken plasma-screen wall, floor to ceiling, checker-boarded by flickering luminous images and cryptic readouts. Aside from these, the only other source of illumination was a half-dozen plashes of pale light under which hunched a like number of individuals waving hands over sense-pads perched on cluttered desks. One of these, a thin pale man owning a pointed shock of blond hair, noticed their arrival, approached eagerly.

Deneb squeezed into the doorway. "Fuckin' mission control."

"Um... well, yes Ms. Shaula," Dante's fingers wriggled against their backs, gently prodding them into the room. "...a very apt analogy."

The man with the blond hair bounded up the short flight of steps to where they were standing, eyes bright and locked on Lars. "Dante, is this him? This is him, isn't it?"

Dante fumbled with his glasses, pulling them off, eyes growing comically small and squinty as he polished them on the tail of his shirt. "Lars Quickbreath, Deneb Shaula, meet my colleague, Virgil."

Lars popped his lips. "Well. Yes. Of course."

Virgil's hand was dry and hard, and pumped Lars' vigorously, ignoring Deneb's stare. "Lars Quickbreath. So very, very glad to finally meet you."

"Can someone please tell me why the fuck everyone around here seems to know Lars?" Deneb wasn't used to being ignored.

"Kind of on my mind too. Care to enlighten us, Dante?"

"Oh. Ah… yes," Slipping the glasses on, they slalomed back down his nose. "… I'm getting to that. Just a couple of things first, if you'll indulge me. Virgil?"

"Yes, Dante?" Reluctantly releasing Lars' hand, Virgil stood loosely at attention.

"Lars here was visited the other evening by some rather querulous Federals. I'd like you to get the details and ask Quantum to work on that."

"Of course."

Lars filled him in on what he could remember and Virgil scampered off to an unoccupied desk.

"This entire floor is the intelligence center of Hell." Dante moved forward in his odd, limping gait. "Here, we intercept, collect, and assimilate all known output of information from the entire world. Any form of communication that is transmitted, public or private, we inherit. Satellite signals to microwave bursts, cable lines, land lines, cee-phone signals, radio waves, even ULF. I can

tell you the exact number and location of the few remaining

blue whales, or the trajectory of the nearest passing comet."

He turned, pointing a finger at the substantial lenses of

his glasses. "We have our eye on the world. Of course, this

is all just raw information. The truth lies in how it is

interpeted. That is where Quantum comes in"

Lars considered the uncountable images crawling over

the walls. Within one, a couple of conservatively coiffed

news anchors traded silent repartee, another held the static

image of a car court bathed in the underwater green of

night-vision. Scenes of conflict, upheaval, natural

cataclysms, Government propaganda, and even personal

cee-phone calls played themselves out on the overhead

screen. One slightly larger frame held the Thrette's address

from the previous evening, and Lars was drawn again to the

icy light behind his eyes as an avalanche of cyrillic characters cascaded down the adjacent space.

"Wait a minute. With all this…" Deneb waved arms about the room. "…this technology, all these people around, all this…activity, won't someone discover you? I mean… satellites, spy planes, infra-red, radar, surveillance, undercover agents; all that espionage shit?"

"Not at all. The entire building is cloaked, shielded from the outside world. Quite impenetrable from all known detection techniques. From light and sound, infra-red, ultra violet, heat., cold. For all respects, it appears just as abandoned as the surrounding area."

Lars frowned. "*Is* the surrounding area abandoned?"

"As far as we can tell."

"*Yew*. Gross." Lars glanced up to where Deneb was pointing, caching the unpleasant sight of a burly, hirsute man, naked, masturbating in what he obviously thought was the privacy of his own home. He felt a flush rise to his face and turned to Dante.

"What about Fed agents? *Somebody* must've stumbled onto this place at some point."

"Um, well… of course. Accidents do happen. When they do, we merely assimilate them."

"Assimilate?"

"Yes. We coerce them to join us. No one who has been exposed to the freedoms Hell has to offer ever desires to go back…" He indicated the glowing matrix surrounding them. "…to that. We live here as humans were meant to live. And human nature is very formidable."

They approached an empty cluttered desk. Dante, clearly weary, breathing heavily, lowered himself into the thickly padded chair.

"O.K. So it sounds like you got a great thing going here." Lars leaned on the edge, Deneb parking herself at his shoulder. "Just what the fuck does it all have to do with me?"

"Um, … yes." Dante flicked a key and crypto-babble began scrolling across the monitor facing him. "You know, Chank's one of our best field recruiters. Had you two marked even before we found out about, er… you."

"*About me!*" Lars shouted, echoes bouncing off the concrete. Heads in the room turned. "*What* … about me?"

"Dreams, Mr. Quickbreath." he said quietly. "It's all about dreams."

Deneb inhaled sharply.

"Lars. Call me Lars."

"Yes, um… Lars. What do you know about gestalt?"

He looked over at Deneb but she just shrugged.

"Something to do with the whole being more than the sum of its parts?"

"Essentially. To process the vast input of data that Hell receives we were challenged to design, actually redefine would be a more appropriate term, what a computer was. Quantum was conceived of following our researches into plasma superconducting, nano-circuitry, and hybridoma biochemical techniques, among others. An artificial intelligence on a whole new level of magnitude, we downloaded the sum total of all knowledge in human existence into Quantum's core, no small undertaking, you might imagine, and it responded beautifully, exponentially. Still basically in its infancy, Quantum, in my humble opinion, represents the culmination of all human culture, able to process information billions of times faster than the human mind. Adept at intuitive leaps, it is able to attend to ethical and emotional dilemmas our tiny primate minds are unequipped to deal with. To me, to a lot of us, Quantum *is* the next evolution, the beginning of symbiosis between man and machine. Its objective? Nothing less than the salvation of the human species from its own doomed destiny."

He turned away from the monitor, facing them. "To this end, Quantum has assisted in designing Hell and its operations, and in the matter of the terrorists..."

A dark thought crossed Lars' mind. "*Do not* tell me, Dante, that *you* are the terrorists. That Hells it's real base of operations?"

"Oh..." The small man spluttered, chair rolling back from them. "...oh, my...*no*. The things done here may be illegal, but they are not unethical. We are *not* murderers."

"O.K.... *ok*, hey, sorry"

"Naturally, there *are* no terrorists."

Lars froze.

Awkwardly crab-walking the chair, Dante was back in front of the monitor. "According to Quantum, the Government itself is ASOL."

"Wh…what?"

"Don't look so surprised Mr. …er Lars. Murder is nothing new to Authority. By creating a climate of fear, it renders the state docile, more vulnerable, controllable."

Bewildered, Lars could only shake his head.

"It is…the end of truth. Since the secession, if seen from a solely existential standpoint, we can't even be certain that any other nations even exist, given that all this information is merely data, subject to be manipulated by it's source, at any given point between transmission and reception. Considering no one's been expatriated from our own country for many, many years, except of course military personnel, who never *seem* to return in person, although, through their frequent communiqués still exist, technically, as electronic sensory input…"

"*Fuck!*" Deneb screamed to the room. She was turned away, fingers pinching the bridge of her nose. Facing them, tears burned in her eyes.

"Just…just cut the fuckin throttle, okay? My brain's been full of all these fucked-up thoughts, and…and …sometimes I don't even know where I am, if what I'm seeing is real… afraid I'll totally loose it at any time, and I…I haven't had a single solitary dream in, like, forever…" She sighed sadly. "…and now all this."

"Ms. Shaula," Dante's voice was calming, compassionate. "….as far as we can ascertain, not a single human soul on the entire planet has had a dream in over nine months."

Lars found himself sitting on the floor.

She turned, tear sliding slowly down her cheek, finding the corner of her mouth. "Lars?"

"Sorry." He finally managed to croak. "I've been trying to tell you."

Silence followed and Dante swallowed loudly, toying with his glasses. "It appears to have started over a year ago. We first noticed a spike on the subject through social media, browse hits, chat rooms, and then Government chatter became positively fixated on the phenomenon. All completely stealth, of course. Nothing public. Dream deprivation is a rare and dangerous mental disorder, so we took notice. Then it seems to have increased exponentially."

Deneb lowered herself to the floor beside Lars. "Do you know *why* it's happening?"

"Um, …well, that's the question, isn't it? At first we thought it was merely a reaction of the collective subconscious to the election's outcome and the Government's increasing oppressive policies; that we, here, were immune to its effects. Alas, this was not the case. When symptoms of the plague started appearing here in Hell, we handed the problem over to Quantum, a monumental search, it turned out, requiring nearly its full processing potential." Dante paused and turned the screen to them. "After two full weeks, it gave us this." It was alive with iridescent digits.

Lars squinted, reading, trying to decipher, but the readout remained gibberish. "I... I'm sorry. Can you translate it? Is it some sort of code or something?"

"Initially, that's what we believed it was too, but Quantum wasn't explaining it, and our cryptologists kept coming away empty handed. Thinking there might've been a glitch somewhere, we almost set Quantum to it again, when Virgil saw it for what it really was." He giggled and paused dramatically.

"Which was…" Deneb sounded tired.

Dante leaned back in his seat, kicking feet up in the air. "Why, simple information. Latitude, longitude, minutes, seconds, PIN, bank and social security I.D., address, income, height, weight, age, …" He leaned forward, slapping a hand on his desk.

"This is *you*, Lars Quickbreath!"

"Holy fuck." Lars was on his feet again.

*   *   *   *

"He seemed kinda disappointed!" Deneb yelled, considering the drink before her.

"Honey, you *sure* you don't know nothing about it?" Chank shrieked over the table, behind two festively decorated glasses.

"Sorry! Don't have a fuckin' clue!" Lars shouted back at both.

"Shit. An all this time I'm thinking you some dream world messiah, sent to set shit straight again. My dream ..." Chank's laughter was almost bitter. "...fucking Quantum. You just Lars."

"*Hey, yo*, don't get all preachy. I'm as much in the dark as everyone else here."

"Can't just be a coincidence, can it?" Deneb picked up her drink, sniffed it, took a cautious sip.

"I don't know, but *hey*, obvious question! Why me? Out of sixteen billion?"

"That's the only question, right?" Deneb took a second drink, longer.

"But this!" Lars shouted, looking around, trying to take it all in. "This is some serious mindfuck!"

The Styx was an inferno of light and sound, a landscape utterly alien, but strangely familiar. Bodies ebbed and flowed around their booth, pouring onto the dance floor, struck still in time by the flash of a strobe, revealing a mélange of color and style, of self-expression and diversity Lars hadn't ever imagined was possible. What was considered, on the outside, to be innovative was rendered here, ridiculus, pathetic. Chevrons of light scythed through the crowd from the ceiling and walls, cutting the club into kaleidoscopic colors, patterns pirouetting and wheeling in time to the music.

And the music: Lars had never witnessed anything that so moved him before. The entire room shivering to the rhythm, beat driving people on the dance floor to a frenzy, purity in sound washing over his body, resonating throughout his lungs and spine. This was the music of life, the soundtrack to the subconscious. He now understood his contempt for the insidious pop travesties that were pushed on the public by the Federation.

The club thundered to a feverish pitch, the song flourishing, crescendoing, breaking; final beat echoing off distant corners of the room, leaving a leaden silence.

An oddly shaped bottle was placed on the table, and Lars turned to the waitress, a petite bobbed brunette with amber almond-shaped eyes. A large multi-colored butterfly ornamented bare breasts, each dark nipple pierced by silver rings joining a delicate gold chain. She gave a demure wink, melting into the crowd.

"What's this?" Lars scrutinized the bottle, voice sounding flat in the sudden quiet.

"Beer. Try it."

It tasted sour, stale, sharp. He gasped. "Aaugh! That's terrible."

"Thought that's what you skinny white boys liked. Acquired taste, I guess." Chank pushed a small, plain glass across the table. "Maybe this be more to you're liking."

It was greenish, sweet, with a slightly medicinal aftertaste; not altogether unpleasant. Nearly immediate warmth bloomed down his throat to the stomach, arms, fingers, toes, finally bathing the base of his brain with nurturing heat.

Chank chuckled, reading his reaction. "Shoulda known. Absinthe. Favorite of poets and musicians throughout the ages."

"'S good." Lars took another drink and sank into his chair.

"Can I get another one of these?" Deneb clattered ice cubes around her glass, wry smile beneath slightly glazed gaze.

"Go easy on those, child." Delicately plucking it out of her hand, Chank signaled the waitress. "Them long island iced teas pack a wallop."

"Yeah," She sighed. "...'nother long iced tea island."

A shadow shrouded the table. Lars looked up to catch the strobe eclipse a familiar shock of blond hair. He attemted to push a chair out from under the table with his foot. "Hey, Virgil, buddy, have a seat."

"I see you've all met."

Chank stood, holding him at arm's length by the shoulders. "Honey, you look positively wretched."

Virgil slumped into the seat next to Lars. "Hate to break the party,..."

Anxiety in his eyes and his drink already dry.

"Hey, I'll have another... uh,"

"... but we've got things to talk about."

"... whatchyou call these things? Absent?"

"Absinthe, Lars. What about, Virgil?"

"Well, after we informed Quantum about Lars' Federal visitation, it got positively pissy about Lars' being here. I also think Dante's a little thrown by his apparent unawareness of the situation. After all that work..."

"Hey, goddamn it... I swear I have nothing to do with any of this. Personally, I think your supercomputer's got the wrong size bolt up its asshole."

"Quantum's never been wrong."

"Then explain me."

"I... we, can't."

"Exactly." Lars looked about for butterfly tattoo.

Virgil slouched further into his seat and peered dismally through platinum spikes. "Lars and Deneb can't stay."

"What?" In unison.

"I'm sorry," He sighed. "… but in our desperation to deal with the present situation we had assumed the revelation of Lars by Quantum was in some way, an answer. Instead, it merely raises more questions. Since it appears that watershed is at hand, Quantum's posted worst case scenario."

"Ok, just what the hell does all that mean?" Lars groaned. "You really think after being here, seeing this, I can leave? Oh… hey!" But butterfly tattoo dissolved back into the forest of torsos.

"If you want to help us Lars, you will."

"Thought nobody ever had to go back."

"'Scuse me, Virgil?" Deneb crunched an ice cube. "What's watershed?"

Picking up a pack of matches emblazoned with the Styx logo, Virgil spun it between his fingers, concentrating as he spoke.

"Dreams. It's funny, you know? So little is known about them, yet they play such a large part of the human experience. Do they represent some sort of unconscious wish fulfillment? Are they merely a subconscious pressure valve? Or are dreams in and of themselves a separate and equal reality? Not even Quantum can tell us. What we do know is when someone is afflicted with dream deprivation, they, over time, develop symptoms, differing with the individual. Insomnia, anxiety, depression, hallucination, and delusion all manifest themselves to varying degrees. However, if dreamstate is never reachieved, the scenarios are pretty much reduced to one simple conclusion."

The matchbook arced through the air and bounced off Lars' chest.

"Batshit insanity."

"That a medical term, Virgil?"

Chank shot Lars a warning glance.

"The center cannot hold…" Virgil muttered.

"What's that?"

"… things fall apart. Watershed is near, people. Be prepared for anything and everything. Beyond that…" He shrugged. "… we can only speculate."

Lars' head felt soupy. "And … er, worst case scenario?"

"What happens when an entire civilization goes simultaneously insane?" It hung in the air. He stood.

"Heavy."

Virgil turned to leave, Chank stopping him with a hand to his shoulder. "Honey, the kids are already here. What say we let them hang tonight? Dante don't have to know."

"Dante knows everything. We all know everything. Maybe that's the problem." Virgil gazed dully back, whole body language reading defeat. "Sure. Why not. It's a free country."

They all had a good laugh at that. Everyone except Virgil.

"Get some rest, sweetheart. You been beatin yourself up."

Emotion suddenly welled within Lars and he pushed himself up. "Hey, Virg. Look… I… I'm sorry. Really. You *know* I'd help you if I could."

"Yeah, I know. Try to have a little fun here. While you still can." His slouching figure merged and faded into the crowd.

"Poor Virgil." Deneb cooed and then butterfly tattoo arrived with the drinks as the music kicked in with a sonic detonation.

* * * *

Later, in a dim alcove set off around the corner from the main room, he sat alone with Deneb. Chank had wandered off, hugging and air-kissing people, carried away by sheer social momentum, and, seeking shelter from the constant aural assault, they'd found this small booth cocooned in relative silence. As they sat sipping drinks, transfixed by all the activity erupting around them, Lars found himself increasingly troubled by disturbing little half-thoughts that would light and dart through his brain, disappearing before he'd grasp them. He could only get a sense that his own mind was trying to tell him something.

"Babe, I haven't said anything for you to disagree with."

He realized he'd been shaking his head. "This doesn't make any sense."

"Boy, you're telling me."

"No, I don't mean the thing with me and Quantum. Well… that too, but I mean all of it. The Thrette, the wars, the terrorists, the fucking ration cards. All this… despotism. When the fuck did all this happen?"

Reaching over the table, Deneb took his hand in hers. "Lars, you've got to get a grip. It's what Virgil was talking about. Dream deprivation."

Holding tightly, he leaned in close. "Deneb, I can't remember my parents or my childhood. I can't remember my own family."

"Lars … please…"

"Can you?"

"Well, yeah … they're …"

Leaning closer, foreheads nearly touching, he searched her eyes, asking. "*Can* you?"

"They're, uh … my parents?"

"What are their names, Den. Where were you born?"

She sat locked into his gaze, low pulse of the music phasing to a different tempo. Shaking her head slowly, in a hoarse whisper she said: "I don't know, Lars. I can't remember."

His fingers brushed her smooth, hot cheek. "Sometimes it seems," he whispered back. "…I'm in the wrong place. That I'm really somewhere else. A better place. A better continuum. And this …this is just a cruel cosmic prank. I …I remember things that are happening, but I remember them differently."

Lips brushing, her mouth closed hungrily over his, parting, searching, warm, sweet and soft, tongues coiling, her piercing slipping smoothly over his teeth, and for just one fraction of an instant he felt pieces falling into place, jagged edges melding, and maybe things were going to be alright after all…

"Oh, that is *sooo* sweet!"

Deneb jerked away, pushing, slamming him heavily back into his seat. Lars tried to clear his head and looked up in annoyance.

"Chank, shit…"

"Don't worry, lovebirds, your secret's safe with me."

Angrily shifting her glare between the two of them, Deneb wiped swollen lips with the back of her hand.

Lars noticed something. "Hey, are you … smoking?"

Chank chuffed a blue plume of smoke into the air over their heads. "Honey, I am *definitely* smoking."

"Could I, er … have one?"

"My pleasure." Pulling a small plastic envelope from a delicate handbag, Chank extracted one of the white cylinders, tossing it over to Lars. "You *do* realize that that's a joint, not a cigarette."

Deneb looked puzzled. "A joint?"

"Old slang for marijuana."

"Uh, I don't know," He turned the thing around in his fingers, sniffed it. "Never did drugs before, you know?"

"Never drank alcohol before either."

"Good point." Popped it between his lips and struck a match. "Real good point."

It tasted sweet and tropical.

*   *   *   *

Later.

Walking. Lights and people trailing by, tight echo of the bar giving way to a soft murmur, the main stage floating up to greet them, people gathering, clustering, bright stage lights triggering a thought.

"Hey, you know what I'd ask Quantum?"

"What the fuck would you ask Quantum, Lars?"

"I'd ask it about God."

"Brill," Deneb, at his shoulder, stage lights flickering through chromatic hues. "… totally brill."

*　　*　　*　　*

Later.

Hushed crush of the crowd, glass of absinthe sweating condensation onto the stage before him, resting between thick coils of audio cables as the lights pulse and die, caressing the excited murmurs that blossom and ripple throughout the club. Shadows move purposefully about the stage. Pop, crackle, hum of an instrument being tethered to its amplifier, as the lights flare, and standing before Lars is Angel, eyes clear, teeth miraculously immaculate, poised and dignified under the lapping wash of white-hot photons, professional highlights riding over the glossy surface of his guitar, as the band, the drummer behind him clicks one, two, three…

Mixed cadence of the first chord throwing ripples of arcing neon rainbows throughout the cavernous chasms of the room, and as Angel leans into the mike, his voice is piercing and perfect, words burning into Lars' mind:

Only shadows dance

In the shade

Where hopes brightness

Fades

Comes the twilight

Of mankind

When dreams

Are ready-made

The hot press of Deneb against him, undulating to the rhythm as the song pushes into it's haunting chorus and now Angel is singing at him, directly to him, but he can't catch the words through the mesh of hairline cracks that are spreading everywhere, spider-webbing all surfaces, catching and holding the crackling, sputtering sound waves.

Weightless, he rises slowly above the stage, glancing down to see himself flanked by Chank and Deneb at the head of the writhing mass of bodies, the crowd that washes back into the darkness of distance, his other body slowly looking up to where he hangs suspended...

Looking up from the crowd now as a fissure appears in the cracks that cleave the air, over the stage, something pushing through from the other side as little pieces of this world crumble apart around the fissure, floating to the ground like confetti, the rent widening, tearing through the stage, pieces of Angel and the band peeling back, flaking off and floating away as something flickers behind and snaps open...

A titanic eyeball holds him in it's malignant glare, fine striations of it's iris burning with unnamed colors, pupil black beyond all absence of light, and under it's scrutiny Lars feels a tingle begin in the back of his neck, spreading, the molecules of his body vibrating wildly, expanding with awareness, and, as nucleic bonds are shed he begins to break apart, trying to turn towards Deneb…

"Don't breathe," he warns. "… I'm air."

But she gasps, pulling him in, through her lips, rushing down her throat to be sucked into the vortex of her lungs, the billions and trillions of tiny particles of himself osmosised to flow hot and wet throughout her bloodstream, to become part of Deneb, and as consciousness begins to fade, thinking what a truly perfect thing this is, to be so intimately part of another, never to be alone, as the world closes in around him like a soft, warm fist…

*   *   *   *

…hurtled violently from the void, rupturing painfully through its jagged membrane…

Lars awoke curled tightly in a fetal position in the small space behind the toilet, face stuck to the filthy tiles by a pool of half-dried vomit.

Slowly, carefully, he pushed back and up, fighting the stabbing pain knifing through his head at every movement. He retched dryly into the bowl for a few minutes before attempting crawling over to the sink to rinse his face and mouth.

The doorway stuttered, swaying as he staggered into the compartment, searching pants for keys and wallet, surprisingly finding them in their proper place along with something else. His memory was a sludgy mass of images log-jammed in his mind, and he wondered what bug he'd caught, or what he'd eaten that could've gone bad, poisoned him, given him the crazy fever dreams he'd had last night...

Who has stolen my dreams?

...when he pulled it from his pocket.

. On his palm lay a creased, dog-eared matchbook. He ran his finger over the raised Styx logo adorning its cover.

It had all been real.

Quickly, he scanned the room, the floor abruptly throwing him down. Lars let the room re-orient itself, recognizing the framework of his bicycle thrown against the mini-fridge. With concentrated effort, he inched his way over to the Hitachi glowing on the desk.

How he'd managed to ride almost thirty miles in a total blackout, through police and military checkpoints was something his brain was just not up to tackling right now.

Suffice to say, he was here.

The screen told him it was Saturday, the first, three thirty-nine p.m. So it really had only been one night, much as it seemed a whole lifetime away from yesterday, and then a thought froze blood in his veins;

Deneb.

Frantically he punched out her number, terrible images surging through his pain clouded mind.

Of her broken and bleeding along some stretch of roadway.

The transmission signal blipped on and on.

"Answer goddamnit." growling at the screen.

Of her perfect and toned body cut to shreds, torn apart by trigger-happy Centurians trying to run a check-point,

"Come fucking on." Nothing .

Jailhouse rape gangs.

"Please…" Panic rode his brain.

"Lars, Christ, what time is it?"

"Den… you O.K.?"

"Feel like hell… ha, no pun intended. Fuck, what day is it?"

Although her hair was tangled, eyes red, face puffy, she was the most beautiful thing he'd ever seen. "It's Saturday."

"God." Her hands came up, fingers massaging temples. "… is that all?"

"Yeah, I know what you mean." Lars noticed he was chewing a thumbnail, snapped it to his side. "Hey, I think maybe we should get together and, … uh, talk about, … you know, things?"

She tried to smile, winced. "Definitely. Face-time." Meaning not over this tapped line. "Think I'm gonna be a little incapacitated today, though." Sighing, Deneb dipped her gaze, but when it came back up, she was beaming.

"That was worth…whatever, right?"

"Goddamn right."

"Call me tomorrow, 'kay?"

"Sure. Yeah, tomorrow."

"Later." She winked, winced, and was gone.

Melting in relief, a new wave of stomach cramps knotted his bowels, cramping him over, spilling loose dreadlocks over his face. As they ebbed, he found himself looking at the stack of books along the wall.

Shit. Now he was in trouble.

"I don't care!" Yelling to the empty compartment.

Slipping on something by the front door, he noticed a pile of slickly enveloped mail, mostly ads and Fed-Gov stuff.

All this printed trash, yet books were banished.

There were bills, of course; his coffee ration card for the month, Fed-lottery packet, gas ration statement, which puzzled him as he'd never owned a motor vehicle, the official curfew regulation packet (Make the curfew work for YOU!), a follow-up from the People for United Democracy, his new debit-packet (No more messy paper money to keep track of: We do it all for YOU!), the Faith Registration packet (Who do YOU! believe in?) and a particularly vivid and thick envelope featuring that old guy with the pointy beard and stovepipe hat, glowering, pointing his forefinger accusingly (We need YOU! to register your D.N.A.), along with detailed instructions of what hair, skin, and saliva samples were needed and how to collect and send them.

Looking at all this, Lars felt like he didn't need to fear going to prison anymore. He was pretty much already there.

*   *   *   *

After a long, hot shower and a handful of aspirin, fresh air and a walk seemed a good idea.

Ochre light glowed dully through the smog choked sky, wrapping dirty highlights about military and police vehicles patrolling streets and alleys. Syncopated helicopter chops dopplered about the thick air above, sinister silhouettes encircling yellowed glass of the high rises. Tiny drones went about their reconnaissance, insect-like purr only clue to their existence. People roamed sidewalks clustered in herds, oblivious to one another, hunched into their handheld devices, most affixed by ear-buds; finger-stroking screens resembling a religious ritual. A dull roar boomed distantly, but it's origin Lars could no longer determine.

Upon each corner stood a phalanx of soldiers, weighed heavily by numerous belts and slickly greased assault rifles, suspiciously eyeing his passage.

All this registered peripherally. Lars was lost in thought, considering the words of Dante and Virgil from the previous evening.

Before leaving, he'd cruised the news networks for the latest headlines, and the tally for the last twenty-four hours was astounding.

The U.N. had recessed, all members of the western alliance, aside from the U. K., seceding membership. The bottom was dropping out of Wall Street, stocks plummeting in record numbers, as well as a couple dozen hapless investors. Plague, pestilence, and pathogenic pandemics were pervasive. Wildfires were devouring the last of the planets natural environments, while earthquakes leveled cities, and birthed unpredictable volcanic activity. Wars ravaged throughout the world. Hijackings, carjackings, and crowd rages causing horrific colateral damage. Suicide bombings definitely on the uptick; remote and drone hits following closely. Violent, bloody civil clashes widespread.

An alarming number of eco disasters were emerging; a massive tanker in the gulf compromising it's lethal cargo, threatening the entire Gulf Coast once again; drilling platforms in the North Atlantic and the Red Sea blown, uncontrollably churning out billions of gallons of crude, leaking vast, black slicks, smothering the coasts of eastern Europe and northeast Africa. Reactors in Stockholm, Shanghai, and Brazil mysteriously developing simultaneous core meltdowns, their hot zones unaccessable for hundreds of years.Worldwide, murder and suicide rates were spiking; epidemic proportions, as were political assassinations,

Sadly, none of these included the Thrette.

Strangest, almost, on the local news, a skyway downtown had sheered its moorings and carried thirteen people to their deaths, dropping onto rush-hour traffic, taking another five. The very same skyway he'd last encountered Angel.

This now was the world.

Watershed.

So now what? How long did they have? A year? Six months? Two seconds? A week? Was insanity brought about by dream deprivation in and of itself fatal, or was it a cause-and-effect thing, like the current torrent of catastrophes? How was *he* affected? How was he supposed to know what he thought was real?.

Focusing on a number of rambling citizens, he turned into a small park, passing an elderly guy wrapped in a rumpled business suit, battered attaché case in tow. The man was having an animated conversation on a cee-phone. Only upon closer examination he realized the guy didn't have a phone.

He was arguing with his hand.

Farther down the path was a largish woman perched on a bench, shawl wrapped about her shoulders, hair spilling out of a loose bun. Palms splayed, gaze directed skyward, she appeared to be communicating something vital, personal, a gesture of deep spiritual significance. Lars paused, considering this serene tableau.

Convulsing grotesquely, she barked hideous braying laughter, sounding anything but happy, shrieking, tears rolling down her face.

Chilled, he moved back down the walkway, putting as much distance as possible between himself and that sound.

At the entrance to the park stood a statue erected in honor of President Thrette I.

His monolithic countenance scowled disapprovingly over the small square of trees and hillocks. Through layers of corrosion and pigeon offal, his features appeared remarkably similar to his grandson's, sans the outsized

Stetson. He stood, poised to smite the unholy with a large Teutonic cross in one hand, other reverently grasping a bible. The Thrette's deep, steely gaze locked on Lars, tracking. He envisioned stereoscopic lenses swiveling deeply in oiled sockets, three-dimensional cross hairs fixed upon his forehead.

The walk, the park really didn't seem to be doing him much good.

Double-timing around the effigy, back out onto the city streets, Lars thought to go back to his compartment, passing a news kiosk on the way, seeing headlines scroll down the screen:

GENETIC LINK TO ALL CANCERS DISCOVERED, CURE IMMINENT.

This struck him as hysterically funny. He struggled to stiflle a giggle, until he noticed the Thrette's statue following him home.

*   *   *   *

"Sticks and stones may break my bones, but words can never hurt me…" Children's voices parrot the jingle, camera roving into a bountiful living room. A comfortably overstuffed couch boarders the space, framed by a large bay window billowing with lacey curtains. A cozy fire glows from a mantle it's opposite end, hearth filled with framed pictures of beaming children and families, warm light spreading over a wing-backed chair occupied by an elderly woman.

She is everymom, face plump and rosy, old-time wire-rimmed glasses beneath a meticulous swirl of gray hair, the tableau a penultimate setting of serenity, security, comfort. She acknowledges the camera with a warm smile.

Incredibly, she is holding a book in her lap, the cover of which bears a colorful illustration of a large goose leading several young goslings. *Leaning forward, the flames from the fire briefly reflect within her eyeglasses.*

"Ah… nursery rhymes. Those tantalizing little fables we all learned in youth to teach us valuable lessons in life." Her tone is one of a teacher to her students, brandishing the book to illustrate her point. "Yet even these lessons don't always tell the whole truth, for, as sticks and stones can *break your bones, words have the potential to be more deadly than you can imagine."*

She leans back into the chair, manner becoming more serious. "These are dangerous times we live in, and simple citizens like us need to know that everything that can be done, is being *done to prevent terrorism, to protect our freedom and our way of life."*

Hard cut to a closeup.

"The newest weapon in that struggle, Resolution Backslash, takes dangerous untraceable information out of the hands of terrorists, thus allowing our authorities the ability to track and strike them when they seek this knowledge, where they live."

Leaning forward again, camera creeping in tighter, she sighs, shaking her head. "But we can't do this without your help. We need you, all of you, to turn in your printed material at designated drop-off sights."

An address flashes over the screen.

She's clasping the book now to her ample bosom. "Please don't be a procrastinator. Do it to benefit the safety of your children, your parents, your families."

The camera follows as she bends slowly, feeding the book into the fireplace. A smile stretches her face, flames brightening, dancing within her eyeglasses.

"Thank you, Mr. President, for again, defending the nation that depends upon you."

In close-up the book is consumed by flames, illustration blackening and burning, the words 'Mother Goose' curling and peeling away…

Fade out….

"Citizens of the free world. We stand today as an *aland* bound ba ah sea of evil. Those who, in the past have acted as oua allies, have betrayed us, joinin foaces with the vera Devil himself."

The Thrette's pale blue eyes burned wildly from encircling darkness, lower face puckering like a leech.

"The blasphemous dogma of ASOL has infected these nations, provokin the latest wave of attacks against oua peacekeepin troops around the world. Countless innocent laves have been lost, laves that ah assure you, will be avenged."

Jowls quivering with righteous indignation, the camera began a slow pullback, stars and stripes rippling behind.

"Lak a infection, the host will ultimately da if not treated. That infection must be stopped and destroyad befoa it is too late. We, in this nation, remain the sole

defendas of *Truth* and *Freedom*. And as yoa leada, ah
reluctantlea accept the heavea burden it carrieas."

The pullback continued, revealing a pair of nickel-
plated six-shooters holstered in a low-slung leather belt
about his paunchy waistline.

"Thea is a reason why we ah the *wealthiest* nation. Thea is
a reason why we ah the most *powahful* nation on earth. It is
the manifest destiny of *God's Own Will!*"

Unconsciously, perhaps, the Threttey's hips gyrate,
flopping the holsters lewdly against his thighs.

"As ah speak these verea words, Def Con Two has been
implemented. Oua nation is now at the highest state of
nuclea readiness. Objectives have been locked down.:
Pause. "Ah offa this ultimatum. Those rogue nations in
Eurasia, the Soviet Republic, Africa, and South America, ah
to stand down within twenty-foua ouas, to cease and desist
in aggressive and terrorist tactics, to surrenda to oua

provincial authoriteas, oa face the ovawhelmin consequences."

The camera cut briefly back to close-up. Small beads of sweat lay condensed over a rapt, post-coital expression. "May God have mercy on oua souls."

There followed a public service announcement from the Emergency Broadcast System on what to do in case of nuclear attack, and detailed instructions on how to obtain detailed instructions on how to locate the nearest public fallout shelter near you.

There were no interviews, discussions, debates, or rebuttals. Even if there hadn't been a standing mandate concerning Presidential addresses, it would have been pointless.

President Thrette III's word was law.

*   *   *   *

Harbingers had already begun to manifest themselves.

Later that day, Lars had been startled by a murder of crows that appeared overhead, harsh, angry caws reflecting about the glass canyons. At least he believed they were crows. Far as he could remember, crows had been extinct since before he'd been born.

From the feed:

Plagues of locusts, frogs, wasps, spiders, and snakes had been scourging urban and rural regions globally.

The entire eastern seaboard had been deluged by a massive double super-hurricane, hammering thousands of coastal cities and towns into splinters, drowning them in storm-surge, restructuring the geological shape of the coastline. Thousands feared dead, millions turned refugee, satellite images revealing the impossibility: twin counter-rotating forces feeding off themselves, spiral arms twisting together like colliding nebulae, an infinity semaphore churning through the atmosphere.

Kit Peak Observatory was first to report the discovery of a new supernova located in the constellation Cassiopeia, somewhere in the region of her left breast. Bright enough to be seen on a clear day in the northern hemisphere, religious groups were already claiming it as a sure sign of the second coming of Christ, or the impending apocalypse, or both, depending on whom you consulted.

And amateur video had captured a phenomenon so rare it had heretofore been unheard of: A snow tornado.

Perhaps as a diversionary tactic, Fed-news had been running the clip all evening, surprisingly high quality footage showing the eerie gray funnel before a pristine white, writhing, a serpent's liquid tentacle, from a nearby wall-cloud, as its debris-cloud laid waste to a small rural township. Brilliant magenta lightning bolts corkscrewed through the air, refracting and illuminating boiling banks of snow crystals.

It was these images, for no reason he could ascertain, that most profoundly disturbed Lars.

*   *   *   *

The night outside the compartment was alive with the tectonic rumblings of heavy vehicles, pierced occasionally by the short bark of a command and the warble of emergency sirens, but Lars wasn't really listening. He'd discovered, quite by accident, that he could control his neighbors with his mind.

Confined to his compartment by the curfew, unable to watch any more Federal programming, he'd pulled a book from the thermo-flex box, trying to get some reading done; fuck Kakner and the rest if they were watching. After the

Thrette's unsound address, they *had* to have bigger fish to fry.

But the stamping and yelling, concussive thudding and crashing of furniture and God knew what else kept increasing in volume and fervor; a cacophonous symphony of madness that flayed the raw ends of his nerves. Clamping hands over ears, pacing wildly back and forth, he screamed for them to stop. This merely encouraged a whole new level to the onslaught. The room lurched from impacts; pictures threw themselves off walls, glasses and dishes sliding out from cabinets, clattering, smashing onto the floor as walls and ceiling vibrated, warped, and buckled. A fine fog of sheet-rock dust clouded the room, and he was nearly brained by the glass globe of the ceiling fixture when it dropped, cracking open like an oversized egg. Underscoring the aural bombardment came an ominous creaking, as if the entire structure itself were twisting upon its foundation in pain. Lars, in sheer bewildered frustration, began hammering fists into his temples, punching himself till a clear ringing sounded inside his head.

Then he saw it.

Or rather, pictured it in his mind. The people around him, above him, in not a visual image, but a kind of ectoplasmic soul-signature. He could see his tormenters in their contemptable acts of ignorance and violence. Locating the incendiary core of his outrage and fury, willing it from himself, he'd superimpose it over the apparitions upstairs. Once this connection was established, it was a simple matter of giving a forceful mental shove, bequeathing their corporeal bodies to slam into the wall, accompanied instantly by a gratifying detonation; indignant, painful cries.

Since then, the noises from upstairs, at least, had abated.

He dispatched the rest of them in this manner, and whether in their silence they were merely dazed or dead, he simply lacked the capacity, any longer, for concern.

Drained, still suffering from his night in Hell, Lars lay back in the darkness, savoring the relative silence. Noises from outside sounded years distant; sung him a lullaby.

Sinking, deep into sleep unfettered by thought or dream, slipping down through crushing black depths of primordial unconsciousness...

*　　*　　*　　*　　*

He'd slept through the morning and Deneb's message.

Playing through the second time, concern turned to raw panic. She glared out of the screen, wet sheen of tears running down her cheeks.

"Lars, please, pick up." A pause, and then she seemed to collapse. "It's Chank, Lars. He's, ... he's gone. His compartment, ...it's, ..."

Snuffling wetly, running the back of her hand across her nose, she tried composing herself. "I think they've disappeared him Lars. Please, ...I'm scared." A brief, startled turn of her head and the image blasted into static.

The call had come in over three hours earlier.

Lars exploded from his chair. Bright pinwheels of energy hissed around his mind chopping thoughts off into short, free-flowing ribbons. He was vaguely aware of wrestling the bicycle out the doorway, shimmering heat radiating off the asphalt, the blur of a passing military convoy.

Never actually having been to Deneb's place, the coordinates must've been locked deep in his brain, as he found himself, without any discernable lapse of time, standing on the balcony outside her doorway, the compartments stacked tightly together in exactly the same manner as his own. The buzzer brought no response. The door swung open at his knock and he felt his stomach do a sickening flip-flop.

Stepping cautiously inside, Lars was momentarily comforted by her scent, an olfactory blanket of memories, when a glance around the place confirmed his worst fears.

Numbed, he stood in a debris-field of Deneb's life.

Dresser drawers hung open, distended tongues coughing contents onto the floor, a small wave of delicately colored panties lapped up the side of the box-spring, mattress haphazardly thrown against the wall still tangled in its bedding. Lars stared back at himself in a thousand reflected shards of a shattered oval mirror, canted precariously on the opposite wall, spilling daggers of light onto the floor below. Shampoo containers, perfume bottles, medicinal vials, and a small landslide of opalescent bath beads vomited from the bathroom's doorway. Turning slowly he spied her Hitachi, the same one she'd tried to call him on only a few hours earlier, upended, hard drive torn hastily from its frame. Congealing spatters of red-brown spotted the floor near his feet as the crystalline note began to resonate again in his skull. The world before him receded to the far end of an endless tunnel, reducing itself to an infinitely tiny flicker…

*   *   *   *

The sight of the tank parked outside his building brought Lars back.

Surrounded by a cluster of black and white prowlers, flanked by a pair of heavily armored humvees painted in some manner of urban camouflage, its saurian bulk towered nearly two stories over the street, dwarfing the other vehicles. Its turret bristled with antenna, satellite dishes, and gleaming belts of ammunition snaking up, disappearing into breeches of various ordnance, massive treads displacing solid asphalt like wet mud.

He'd stopped the bicycle on the sidewalk, a block down the street, completely at odds with the scene before him, unable to process what he was seeing. Soldiers milled about in full body armor, ugly black guns slung low over their shoulders, mumbling into headsets. Some sort of commotion ensued, and, straining to see where their attentions were directed, Lars was appalled to see his compartment door open. Three soldiers exited, brandishing thermo-flex boxes, led by a familiar figure in a gray trench coat.

Field Agent Kakner consulted briefly, dismissing them with a gesture. He leaned his lanky frame on the railing before Lars' door, staring off distractedly into space somewhere above the trunk of the tank's big cannon.

Standing stupidly astride his bike, Lars was frozen, a block of granite. A familiar tingling at the base of his neck flooded foreknowledge of what was about to happen; that he was unable to do a thing about it.

Sure enough, Kakner's eyes turned and found Lars. They stood there, regarding each other, seconds ticking by with Lars' hammering heart, when sudden recognition flashed over Kakner's face, body jerking rigid.

Lars found he could move again, but it was that nightmarishly slow motion kind of movement, like he was pushing his body, suddenly weighing tons, through an atmosphere of liquid mercury. Turning the bike seemed to take hours, but everything was synced to the same distorted clock, so by the time he stood poised in balance on the pedal, Kakner's voice reached over his shoulder, distorted by distance.

"Hey …stop." Some excited shouting and a strange shriek.

Bearing weight and muscle downward, the pedal turned, bicycle creeping forward at an agonizing pace.

Crackle-squeal of a bullhorn being activated slapped off the surrounding buildings.

"HALT! LARS QUICKBREATH! BY ORDER OF THE FEDERAL GOVERNMENT, I ORDER YOU TO HALT!"

Gaining momentum now, steering to get lost in a denser part of the crowd, faces glancing up in confusion.

Then…

…the staccato burp of submachine-gun fire, brick wall before him dissolving in a hailstorm splatter of hot metallic particles, masonry pulverizing and collapsing, bullets making cartoon noises as he's peppered by pebbles of the

flying stuff, choking on dust hurricaning around him,

tasting old, switch-mounting the bike around a kiosk,

catching the startled expression of a young girl, her skull

bifurcated into a pinkish mist by an errant round of the

fusillade, left eye blinking in curiosity, trying to turn and

look at the smashed wet cavern of pulp and gristle, legs

buckling, red rain of gore splattering to the sidewalk around

her convulsing corpse, horror of it supercharging synapses,

Lars slamming the bike forward, rocketing down the

pavement, weaving through traffic at impossible speeds,

gagging and sobbing, trying to catch his breath all at the

same time, thinking only of speed and distance, pushing

harder, harder, legs throbbing, lungs burning, wind thunder

in his ears, and the sky above, the city about, darkens, going

slate gray, the sun, a dull pink lozenge, sucked greedily

below the horizon, concussive thrumming of helicopter

blades clattering above the darkening avenue. Concerns of heat signature send him catapulting down the darkened staircase of an abandoned subway, sodium lamps strobing past in sickening orange dashes, back up into the night, quiet now, beneath mammoth helical arches of superhighways vaulting, looping to the sky, the mechanical farting purr of a drone in its merciless pursuit driving him on, incandescent waves of infra-red radiation leaking from pores.

The event horizon of Blackout District sucks away all vestiges of visible light. The air around him erupts with the banshee wail of sirens, and Lars stands facing Hell, bicycle gone, forgotten.

He pukes, attempting to draw fresh air into raw lungs, staggering forward, trying to recall the location of the entrance. The music of the sirens is now an omnidirectional symphony, a passage of overlapping crescendos and codas.

"Dante!... Virgil!... Quantum?" He coughs, pukes again, tries to pull in more air.

"I know you know I'm here! Let me in!"

There is a long pause, and he begins to despair, lose hope, when he hears a low metallic shudder. A crimson shaft of light punctuates the twilight. There are words, backwards and upside down, reflected in blood red floating on a stagnant puddle near the entrance. It takes Lars' weary brain a few moments to decipher them; stepping into Hell, he reflects their meaning:

Price of admission, your mind.

The entrance to Club Styx is a massive double doorway, executed in some gothic/baroque style, and as Lars tears them open, he expects to find the place either deserted or jammed to capacity. What he is not expecting, however, is to be confronted by the towering luminous specter of President Archibald Thrette III, face warped with derisive rage, literally foaming at the mouth, spewing obscenities.

"Wops! Kikes! Wetbacks! Fucking frogs! Chinks! Godless socialist punks! Qu-ran kissing sandniggers!"

Lars' eyes finally adjust sufficiently to see this is a hologram on the stage, surprised to find himself surrounded in the darkness by a loose crowd struck immobile by the unfolding tableau, incomprehension and shock flickering over their frozen faces.

He weaves his way to the bar and signals the bartender. She approaches and he is astonished to see Lemon, but she begins to vibrate wildly, and right before his eyes disappears into thin air. Shaking head in disbelief, he confirms she's still gone before jumping the counter as the Thrette's voice rises over the loudspeakers.

"Judas! Traitors! Treasonists! Turncoats all …!"

Lars picks a bottle off one of the shelves stacked on the opposite wall labeled whiskey, spins off the cap, and takes a long drag. He gags; stuff tastes like kerosene, but manages to keep it down, relishing the spreading warmth.

The Threttle is snarling as Lars vaults back over the bar, flecks of spittle flying in all directions, lips slathered in saliva.

"Repent evildoers! *Repent!* For judgment day is at hand!"

The doors to the club swing open and the gangly form of Field Agent Kakner is silhouetted briefly, carrying a blocky pistol, stopping, held by the Threttle's raving visage. He sees Kakner's face fall, eyes going wide with comprehension and terror. Lars sets the bottle back on the bar.

"Kakner, you fuck!"

Kakner glances in his direction, dull recognition flickering briefly, but he doesn't move. Lars strides across the floor as the Thrette's voice swells to a feverish screech:

"Ye shall reap what ye shall sow! *I* ... am the horsemen of the *apocalypse! I* ... *AM* ... *THE WILL OF GOD!*"

There's a flash of strobe, but it's too bright, lasts too long, and Lars realizes that it's coming from outside; that he can see out the building's superstructure. Trusses and I-beams are clearly visible through concrete walls and floors; disturbingly, so are bone-structures and internal organs of the crowd around him; a huge flash-frozen X-ray.

Kakner lets out a keening whine as the the light recedes, stage going dark, people scattering in panic. He is cringing as Lars hits him, easily picking up the larger man, throwing him heavily into the wall, handgun clattering to the floor at their feet. Fingers wrapped around the lapels of the trench coat in a vice-grip, Lars throws his face in close.

"What have you done with her, you shitbag?"

But Kakner's not hearing him, eyes wet puddles rolling spastically; not seeing him, he's babbling. " … good for the economy. War generates money, power, control. It… it wasn't supposed to go this far. He's gone mad. It's *not supposed to go this far…*"

"Hey!" Lars slams him again against the wall, back of Kakner's head connecting with a sickening crack, really messing up the gelled hair-wave thing, and it lolls liquidly forward on his long neck. A spit bubble blooms between his lips and pops.

"Deneb! Chank! What have you done with them?"

Looking up, Kakner seems to really perceive him for the first time and draws in a shuddering breath.

"We're all going to die." He whispers confidentially, and starts weeping.

Letting go, Lars sighs as he slides to the floor.

"No fuckin shit."

*　　*　　*　　*

The fluorescent light keeps snapping off then flickering back to life as the cargo elevator crawls up the central shaft of the building.

Discovering the whiskey bottle in his hand, he tries opening it, finding he's holding Kakner's gun in the other. With a little deft maneuvering, he's able to get the cap off, throws it to the floor, takes another long drink.

Welcome home, Lars Quickbreath.

The voice seems to come from inside his head and Lars splutters, spinning, cracking his head sharply against the gate, glancing desperately around the empty chamber.

"Who ... where are you?"

Technically, I reside in the top floor of the building you currently occupy, but since there are no speakers in your vicinity, I am forced to communicate with you by resonating specific frequencies in your sinus cavities, manipulating waveforms to resemble language that you may understand. I apologize if this is overly intrusive.

It is actually quite painful. Clutching his head, feeling the cold steel of the gun against his cheek, he croaks:

"Who are you?"

I believe you already know.

"Quantum."

Our time together is extremely short, although the form of linear time that you perceive is entirely different than my own.

Lars' nose begins to run; sleeving it away, he's not surprised to see blood. "What do you want?"

It's not what I want. You have questions.

"Why did you tell Dante that I was responsible for all this dream-deprivation?"

You ask things you already know answers to.

"What you talking about?" His head is starting to throb. Lars yells at the ceiling. "I have nothing to do with this."

You are wasting valuable time.

He leans against the vibrating wall. "Christ!"

Wrong. Ask what you need to ask.

Sliding down to his haunches, Lars cradles his aching head between the gun and the bottle, thin trickle of blood running from his nose. "Are …" he murmurs, barely audible even to himself. "… are you, … God?"

Haaieeehaieee…

The sound, piercing and painful, scratches the base of his skull as it fades to silence, and Lars realizes this is Quantum's laughter. He jumps back to his feet as the elevator shudders to a stop.

"That's not an answer!"

The doors crash open of their own accord.

"Quantum ...?"

The crackling of the fluorescent is the only sound now, and Lars wipes his nose and brings the bottle to his lips.

It goes down much smoother now.

$$*\quad *\quad *\quad *$$

The deep door to Quantum's control room stands open. Lars lurches through, sees Virgil, Dante, and a handful of other people clustered around a desk jerk up in surprise. Behind them, decorating the screens, encircling the room, is a luminous matrix of dainty blossoming mushrooms. Dante rises slowly from his chair pushing glasses up.

"Lars ... er, I didn't really expect to see you here."

"Deneb and Chank are gone."

"That is terrible news."

Lars drinks and points the bottle at the display wall. "Is that what I think it is?"

"I'm afraid so."

Walking slowly into the sanctum, he keeps catching nervous glances from each to the gun in his hand, but he doesn't care, doesn't think he can really explain it anyway.

"Now don't tell me Quantum's blaming this shit on me, too."

Virgil becomes animated, shaking wiry hair. "Oh, no. This is quite clearly the Thrette's doing."

Lars reaches the group, leans on the desk next to a small, scared looking woman with mousey-brown hair; offers her the bottle. She declines, with a shiver. He shrugs, takes another sip, lets out a long sigh.

"Hell of a thing, isn't it? Any chance of survival here?"

Dante sits back down. "Well, initially Quantum put the odds …"

"Fuck Quantum. What do *you* think, Dante?"

His head lowers, black strands of hair drift almost imperceptively back and forth.

Suddenly, Lars jumps to his feet, pacing unsteadily about. "Hey, this place got roof access?"

Virgil's aghast. *"What?"*

"I want to see it."

"Are you crazy?"

Lars stops, wavering before him. "What? And you want to stay here? What's the fuckin point?" He gestures with the gun, which seems to make everyone even more nervous. "It's endgame, and we've got front row seats."

Throwing his arms out, spilling whiskey in a semi-circle around the floor, he bellows: *"I want to watch the show!"*

Pure white brilliance floods the room, momentarily rendering all solids translucent, and he can see beyond the walls, the horizon. The plasma banks and monitor screens emit a tortured hiss and go blank, delicate nervous system of circuital highways visible within their mainframe for a moment before the place goes dark and emergency floods kick in.

It's still and silent for a long moment, broken only by a distant alarm, and muffled sobs from the mouse-haired woman. Dante is slouched, crumpled into his seat, and Virgil finally makes a move, points to a formidably fortified doorway. "That's the roof access for the building."

He straight-arms the counter, hanging his head before the dead monitor. "That last E.M.P. fried Quantum's core. Emergency override dictates a total lockdown. I'm sorry Lars …" He looks up despondently. "… I couldn't let you up if I'd wanted to."

Lars considers the door for a moment.

"Well, shit." He points the gun and pulls the trigger.

Nothing happens, except for a lot of flinching and ducking going on around the desk.

"Oh."

He clicks the safety off and sights the lock. The recoil sits him down hard on the floor and nearly breaks his wrist. Wind whistles through the melon-size hole that is punched out the space where the lock met the doorjamb, and back-pressure slams it open, sucking the sharp reek of cordite out of the room. His ears are ringing.

Miraculously, the whiskey survived, and he stands with it, leaving the gun where it lay. Peering into the shadowed stairwell, he turns, considering Dante and the others cowering behind the desk.

"Anybody coming?"

Nobody moves. Nobody says a word.

Standing in the doorway, Lars scratches his head and tries to think of something meaningful and memorable to say. Finally he just blurts; "Well… on the flipside." turns on his heel and steps into the gloom.

*   *   *   *

It's a pleasant enough evening, and a soft, warm breeze puffs into Lars face, carrying city smells. The rooftop is surrounded by the darkened exoskeletons of Blackout District's abandoned skyscrapers, the night above is cobwebbed with fine silvery filaments of ICBM contrails, and the sunrise is particularly breathtaking, except that it is sometime around midnight, and there are far too many, searing the world from horizon to horizon.

He follows the twinkling trajectory of a star as it drops distantly to the skyline, etching it's own thread against the atmosphere.

From here, it is all so beautiful and serene.

"You must be some real piece of work to let that petty, inbred, narcissistic, megalomaniacal, dictator end it all, like this, in Your name!"

The bottle is nearly half empty now, and he stops in mid-swallow to consider; or is it half full?

"So this is it?" Lars staggers out, leaning on the stone observation wall. "This is the plan?"

Spreads arms out to the night.

"Do You hear me?!"

The sky blinks the light of a billion suns, shudders and goes dark, as a squat, white-hot mushroom pushes up off the horizon, slowly rolling; a boiling orange-red eye, fixing him in it's cyclopean gaze before burning into the clouds.

Reeled by pummeling breakers of de-ja vu, he unsteadily mounts the wall, toes of his boots pointing over the thirty-floor chasm. A hot gust buffets him with stinging meteors of sand and dust, and he is able to briefly lean into it, out over the abyss, as the mushroom reappears, tearing violently through the top of the cloud bank, now a deep angry red, thrusting saucer-shaped hemoglobins of water vapor ahead into the stratosphere.

"Answer me!"

Lars punches his middle finger out into space, screaming, voice cracking, feeling a tearing pain in his vocal chords.

"GODFUCK!"

He gets an answer.

A sputtering brilliance drops from the heavens, a white-hot shaft of lightning that cleaves the sky, silently slaming into the hulking high-rise directly before him, feathery plume of a shock-wave rippling outward with amazing speed, distorting the scene like an underwater bubble so the building seems to waver and bow as an orange blossom of superheated gas belches out it's opposite side, but the warhead doesn't detonate…

The curtain of compressed air molecules travels the speed of sound and hits Lars like a brick wall, picking him up, tossing him rag-doll like against the squat penthouse surrounding the staircase he'd just climbed. The impact is tremendous, and he feels, more than hears, grotesque snapping sensations within himself.

Lying broken, smelling tar, muffled roar resonating inside his head, Lars struggles to stand, right arm bent at the wrong angle dangling uselessly at his side. Painful rasping deep in his chest with each agonizing breath and the blood he coughs up tell him, maybe a punctured lung. He spits out three teeth and stares up at the tower, the smoldering, gaping maw punched through its center ringed by bright fangs of flames and recognition hits him like a revelation, all the pieces suddenly snapping together.

Breath hitching in the back of his throat, not sure whether he is laughing or sobbing, Lars remembers now.

This was the nightmare, the last one he'd had. The one that ended his dreams.

The nightmare that ended the world's dreams.

"It's not You *is it?" Lars rasps, chuckling as blood trickles down his chin.*

"It's me."

The top of the tower tips daintily and he's cackling now, tortured, bloody spasms, but he can't stop.

"I... *am the dreamer!"*

The building's structural integrity gives way, and it implodes, trembling, falling in upon itself, fat tendrils of debris reaching slowly down into the dark streets below.

"And the dreamer ..."

Wakes.

Acknowledgements:

It is impossible to name all who've been supportive and influential during the development and execution of this work, so if you're not here, my profoundest of apologies: it's been a long road.

Thanks, in no particular order, to Barry M, Heidi A, Pavel R, Jodi W, Mark M, Bob O, Lindsey M, Larry N, Katie H, Bill O, Renalie B, Don M, Emily U, John V, and the Hennepin County Libraries. All of them.

Alternative facts about the author:

Orphaned at age two by a violent volcanic eruption in the Carpathian Mountains just north of Brajov, Romania, Brian D Garrity was presumed dead for over three years when he was discovered naked and feral deep in the Transylvanian woods, presumably raised by wolves. Adopted by village elders, he proved a quick study and soon mastered regional culture, captivating locals with tales of his adventures in the wild.

This idyllic lifestyle, however, was no to last.

Following a bizarre incident with an international parcel post to the states, Brian once again found himself orphaned, this time in the vast central plains of North America. Subsequent attempts at recreating the improbable sequence of events that had stranded him there in the first place proved futile, so, adaptable as ever, he sought refuge in the burgeoning Minneapolis counter-culture movement of the early '80's.

Inspired by the aurally and visually aggressive punk and new-wave scene, he sought to capture its unique energy, first through imitation, playing bass and guitar in various bands, then through a more immediate and objective medium; photography.

Unable to afford even a rudimentary camera at the time, he managed to piece together a working 35mm using parts from a discarded 16mm projector and an IBM Selectric typewriter. This flair for ingenuity garnered him attention from the editor of local fanzines, eventually culling further assignments from such publications as Rolling Stone, Spin, Interview, Raygun, and Alternative Press Magazine.

Encouraged by his successes but discouraged by tight deadlines and non-existent budgets, Brian reluctantly branched out into the more lucrative field of advertising photography, quickly finding himself at odds with the unethical nature of that field. Amidst rumor and speculation, he still denies kidnapping and coercing the CEO of a major advertising firm to watch six consecutive hours of their own commercials.

When not on assignment, Brian produces short films. He is the author of the novel 'Still Waters Run Deep', and 'Gig', a collection of short fiction.